INDOMITABLE
The Last Ditch

Matthew Willis

© Matthew Willis 2021.

Matthew Willis has asserted his rights under the Copyright, Design and Patents Act, 1988, to be identified as the author of this work.

First published in 2021 by Sharpe Books.

CONTENTS

The Calm
The Storm

INDOMITABLE

The Calm

27 July 1942

The hook caught the Jesus Christ-wire, snapping the excuses out of Edmund's head. A lance of pain and he was holding hot, salty blood in his mouth, half his tongue incandescent.

The Hurricane's tailwheel thudded onto the deck and Edmund swallowed the blood. Remembered to throttle back. Jesus, what just happened? The barrier had been right in front of him, he'd been hurtling towards it as the Hurricane floated over the wires and-

Of course. The PO must have lowered it at the last second. He breathed out through his nose, swallowed more of the fluid iron-salt puddling below his tongue.

Bumps and judders from the fuselage, somewhere behind him deck crew freeing the wire. Already a man on each wingtip. The PO standing by the island, waving him forward. He gunned the throttle, taxied along the pitching deck, bumping over the now-lowered barriers.

His heart was still running away, so hard he could hear it over the engine, so fast he could not make out the individual beats. Jesus, what a mess.

This whole barrier business was new to him. It shouldn't make any difference, but it seemed to pile the pressure on. And just when it was least welcome. *Eagle* and *Furious* hadn't had the infernal things. If you fluffed the landing, you just opened the throttle, and went round again. On *Indomitable*, there were two steel nets stretched across the deck in front of you. Miss a wire and your kite'd get sliced up like a block of cheese. It was bound to make a fellow feel tense. The arrestor wires were closer together than on *Eagle*, too. It took some adjusting to.

That wasn't it. Even as he shut the engine off and pulled the pin out of his harness, he knew that was not the reason he had been flying so badly, and landing like a sprog. It was just another excuse.

There was a clatter on the wing root and Charlie, his new rigger, was there, taking the harness straps and arranging them so he didn't catch himself when he climbed out. "That looked exciting sir. Thought we was going to be peeling you out of the barrier for a moment," he said nonchalantly.

"So did I," Edmund replied, trying not to sound winded.

"CO wants to see you sir. Right away he said."

Edmund clenched his teeth. "I'll bet he does."

Charlie grinned and started whistling.

***

Lieutenant Commander Haddow glanced up from the heap of paper on his desk. "Ah, Clydesdale, come in," he said, his gaze having returned to the paper before he finished speaking. "Bill? Go and get yourself a tea," he called out to his writer, sitting at the desk beside Edmund. Bill darted a look at Edmund, betraying something like pity, and disappeared into the passageway.

Edmund stood for a second. How was he supposed to 'come in' when the entire space in the tiny cabin was taken up by the CO's bed, a small desk next to it and the CO's chair, not to mention the CO? Edmund always felt like a child beside Haddow. He reminded Edmund of a prefect. Edmund was a little shorter than average himself, and somewhat weedy after three weeks on Malta, while Haddow was a big fellow, clumsy and soft in appearance, like a schoolboy who had not quite adjusted to a sudden growth spurt. His expression was anything but soft. "Well, I gave you an order," he snapped. "Come in."

"Aye sir!" Edmund shuffled into the doorway – not that there was a door, even, just a curtain separating the cabin from the outer office. The tips of his toes were just about over the threshold. He put his hand to his head and instantly regretted it. His hair was soaked with sweat, the usual sandy brown colour turned black.

Haddow finished reading the page in front of him, then shuffled round on the chair to face Edmund. "You know what we're here for, Clydesdale?"

Here? As in Freetown? Or as in here on a pretty new armoured carrier training as if it were going out of fashion? The rumours were rife. Amphibious landings in Libya... Another raid on the Italian battle fleet... "I expect it's another convoy to Malta, sir." Expected? Hoped. Malta would fall in weeks if no more supplies reached it soon. And Malta was everything.

Not just for the war effort. For Edmund.

Haddow narrowed his eyes. "You're slurring, Clydesdale. You aren't drunk, are you?"

"No sir!" Edmund yelped, sending a hot dart through his mouth. "Bit my tongue when the hook caught."

"Oh. Well I'm not surprised. Anyway. The coming operation." His eyes narrowed. "What have you heard?"

"Nothing sir!" Edmund spluttered. "I mean to say, I was there. Malta. A few weeks ago. If they don't get supplies soon, we'll lose the island."

Haddow folded his arms. "It's not confirmed yet, but I wouldn't do anything to disabuse you of the convoy notion. Given how aware you are of the importance of such an operation, would you mind telling me what the hell... what *happened* with the training flight?" Haddow's voice was quiet, betraying an effort of will to keep it neutral. Haddow knew damned well. But he was giving Edmund a chance to explain himself.

Or enough rope to hang himself with.

Edmund went through it all, holding up the moments when he might have done something differently for examination. Less for Haddow than for himself. He had screwed up, after all. Explained how quickly the cloud had built as they'd approached the destroyer that was acting as the target ship. How Edmund, leading the escorting fighters, lost the Albacores in the accreting sky-clag. And rather than muck about looking for them, proceeded to the target independently. It might have ended up alright, but he'd failed to find the destroyer in time and before long, the radio filled with the delighted gabble of 880 Squadron, acting as the defenders, who could not believe their luck. *Help yourselves everybody, there's no fighter escort*. It was judged that all the Albacores had been shot down before getting anywhere near the target.

"Hmm." Haddow pursed his lips. Weighing. Analysing. "It was a mess. What should you have done?"

"Stayed close to the bombers, sir." That *was* what he should have done. Should do in future. And yet he would do the same again. He would not knowingly lead men under his command into the risk of a collision.

Not after the last time. Not after his wingman, poor Leonard, bought it.

Edmund kept the thought to himself.

The response seemed to make Haddow even angrier. "Yes. Of course. So why the hell *didn't* you stay close to the bombers?"

"It was getting very thick, sir."

"Thick? Lucky we didn't have you with us on the *Bismarck* show if you think *that's* thick." Haddow exhaled through his nose. A frustrated hiss. "What happens if on this hypothetical convoy, the Italian fleet comes out, and the only thing capable of stopping them is the Albacores *you* just left to get shot to hell?"

Edmund said nothing. It was better that way. Anything that came out of his mouth now would either be unnecessary self-condemnation or pleading. Neither were as dignified as silence.

"And as for that landing," Haddow went on, "half the squadron only have a handful of deck landings on Hurris to their name and you, with a few hundred, were the only one who nearly pulled the bloody hook out! You realise your crate will have to be inspected, don't you? Better hope you didn't overstress the airframe."

"I know, sir, yes."

"You should apologise to the riggers, they've enough work to do as it is."

"I will, sir."

"Bloody right, you will." Haddow looked up again, fixing eye contact, his stare boring into Edmund. "I've heard enough about you from people high and low to make me wonder whether taking you on was worth the bother, but I concluded that it was. Now don't make me wrong, Clydesdale. Do better next time. And don't rely on there being too many next-times if you don't buck your ideas up. We'll be putting into Freetown in a few hours. Go ashore for a bit, sort your head out and come back ready, or you might as well not come back at all. Dismissed."

Edmund staggered down the passageway, uncertain if the unsteadiness in his legs arose from the rolling of the ship or the after effects of Haddow's interview. It was catching up with him. His mistake. His fraud. His lie. He tucked himself into a corner beneath a companion ladder and fumbled in his pocket for the offending paper. What had Haddow said?

...I've heard enough about you from people high and low...

His fingers found the edge of the paper and he tugged at it. The rustle seemed loud enough that it could be heard the length of the ship. He held the crumpled slip before his eyes, like a talisman.

EDMUND STOP TOLD DADDY ABOUT CLAIMS STOP THINK HE REPORTED STOP BARBARA

Told Daddy about claims... In other words, his former girlfriend had told her father – the Assistant to the Second Sea Lord, no less – that his four air-combat victories, the kills (how he hated that word) that had briefly made him a minor celebrity, were all spurious. A combination of accident, politics and cowardice. It would surely make the Fleet Air Arm a joke if word got out.

Was one of Haddow's "people, high and low" in the Admiralty? There was a fair chance of it. Did Haddow know Captain Thomalin himself? Again, a fair chance. And Thomalin had 'reported him'? Who to? Were the papers summoning him to a court martial winging their way from England that very minute? Or was the 'report' to a reporter... Did Thomalin seek to ruin his reputation in the press?

Either way, it seemed his days here were numbered. He'd lied...not intentionally, not maliciously, and yet the lie had got away from him, had been used to glorify the Navy at the darkest moment of the war, and when the lie was discovered, he would have to be made an example of. Haddow's opinion of him could hardly be lower as it was, but even if he avoided a court martial, Haddow would not stand for a person like Edmund in his squadron. No self-respecting squadron commander would. It was probably why his last CO had been so happy to see him transferred, come to think of it.

He closed his fist around the telegram. He'd go back to Haddow now. Tell him all about it. At least then it would be over. The lie would no longer hang over him. Perhaps in time he could make up for it. It wouldn't be in the Fleet Air Arm. At least, not in the cockpit of a fighter aircraft. But there would be something.

Edmund turned on his heel and strode towards Haddow's quarters. He'd barely reached the end of the passageway when he heard his name called, and turned to find his puffing rigger pursuing him.

"What is it Charlie?" Edmund shoved the telegram back

into his pocket, affecting to look casual.

"Wondered if you could spare a minute sir. In the hangar?"

Oh lord, he'd wrecked the Hurricane with that landing, hadn't he? Haddow had told him to apologise to the riggers... now was as good a time as any. And then he'd go to Haddow to confess. "Of course," he said, smiling awkwardly. "Lead on."

Charlie led on, scurrying through passageways and up and down ladders like a monkey.

"Sorry about that landing," Edmund puffed as he attempted to keep up.

"That's alright sir," Charlie replied brightly. "At least you didn't go over the side, eh?"

The thought, which had not occurred to Edmund, and the exertion, half compelled him back into silence. *Indomitable* did the rest. She was about 29,000 tons to Eagle's 22,000, but felt four times as big, ten times as labyrinthine. There was a different sense to her as well. A purposefulness. *Eagle* had never quite shaken off her peacetime manner. The war was something that had happened to *Eagle*. *Indomitable* existed for it. Commissioned in wartime and crewed mostly by hostilities-only types, the war was in her very fabric.

Edmund knew they were getting close when the odd smells of potatoes or burned rubber hanging in corners and lobbies were swamped by the reek of hundred-octane. Before long Charlie was unclipping a door which swung aside to reveal the frenzied hangar.

In a moment they would be in too much noise to speak

without shouting. "So was my kite fixable?" Edmund blurted. "Must be a fair amount of work I put you to."

Charlie just grinned, and stepped into the hangar, waiting for Edmund to follow and clipped the door unhurriedly behind them.

"Oh we could do better than patch up that old wreck sir. We've got you a new one."

"A new one? Where on Earth from?"

Charlie grinned. "Come have a look-see."

They moved past a tangle of Hurricanes, arranged puzzlingly to allow for their non-folding wings. Beyond, at the workshop end was another Hurricane, bright in the grey gloom, among the dull-painted fighters. Land camouflage. It was still in pieces, the wings hung on the bulkhead like trophies.

"Hang on, this is a Mark Two!" Edmund was shouting and already he could barely hear himself.

Charlie nodded. "That's right," he yelled. "Brand new. One of the kites meant for Burma on the last supply run, only the engine went U/S before it took off."

"What's it doing here?"

"Wasn't any way of shipping it back ashore so we struck it down in the hangar. Plan was to use it for spares."

"It's not a Sea Hurricane?" Edmund looked at the rear fuselage. Smooth underside, uninterrupted by a tailhook. How was he supposed to land the thing? He could barely manage when he did have a hook!

"Not yet. But it will be." The rigger pointed to the nearest Sea Hurricane. It was his old one. Already it looked skeletal, all the cowling panels stripped off and a scattering of parts on the deck where they had been carefully, but rapidly, removed. "Chief decided it was easier to rig this airframe up with a hook and spools than to fix your old one. Would have needed to replace a longeron you see, and that's a right b-... That's the devil's own job. Main thing is to swap the engine across – afraid we can't manage a new one of those – and Bob's your uncle. So you've got another four Brownings if you want 'em. Only trouble is she's a little heavier than the others, and you've got no more power, so you might have to flog the engine a bit to keep up in the climb."

Edmund stepped forward, walking around the fuselage, gazing at the wings with an assessor's eye. The nose was a little longer, so it'd be a touch more stable. A fraction less quick to respond in pitch, but less liable to tighten in the turn, easier to hold when turning hard, which would more than offset the disadvantage. And more guns would be welcome. Eight 303s were nowhere near enough these days. Alright then. He'd take the extra weight. Once at patrol altitude it wouldn't matter. This engine wasn't in bad shape compared with some. He could take a chance with the overboost if need be.

If it was anything like Operation Harpoon, there'd be two, three days of intense combat. No sense in being cautious with the equipment. It would be all-or-nothing.

"Knew you'd like it sir!"

"Hmm?" Edmund realised he'd been smiling grimly. He wanted to fly this aeroplane. To see how it felt, to see what it could do. But as soon as Haddow knew about his situation he would surely be stood down from flying...

Charlie was still talking. "...Know the camouflage isn't exactly right, but we should be able to cover the green with a coat of Extra Dark. If you're happy to leave the brown as it is, it's not too different from the slate grey at a distance. We can get that done by the day after tomorrow. By the time we're back at sea it'll be ready to fly. Sir?"

"Yes? Oh, of course. That would do very well."

"Well, there we are then." A moment's relief flickered on Charlie's face. "Happy?"

"Yes. Thank you. Delighted."

Alright. He'd fly the new Hurricane. And confess to Haddow straight after that.

28 July 1942

Freetown. Hot, humid, alive with commotion everywhere you turned. It felt like West Africa concentrated. It was not Edmund's kind of place, but he was happy enough just to be off *Indom* for a few hours. He felt his relief expanding as though it had been released from the steel compartments. He was fairly sure he was lost, and didn't care.

He rounded the corner and collided with a hurtling white-clad form that bounced softly off him and gasped. A dark-banded straw hat fluttered to the ground and he grasped at it just as its owner did the same, pulled it angrily out of his grip and stuffed it back on her head. Nurse, he thought, for a second but then saw the hat had an RN badge on it. The apology was still burbling in his mouth when he looked at the face beneath the hat.

"Bloody hell! *Barbara*?" he yelped. "What! What...!"

Barbara straightened her hat and put her hands on her hips, expressionless, regarding him. "Honestly," she said eventually. "I come halfway to Capetown and the person who knocks me off my feet is...you."

"But what...what are you *doing* here?"

"I should have thought that was obvious, what with me being a Wren and this being a naval base." She tapped the badge on the straw hat.

Edmund resisted the urge to gape. It felt like a dream. Barbara! Here! "When were you posted?" he babbled.

"Got here last week." She looked suddenly decisive, then sheepish, the sharp edges softening. "Look, I know this is a surprise, but do you think we could go and sit down somewhere, preferably out of this racket and infernal blasted heat?"

"Infernal's the word. Only I doubt it's as humid in Hades." Edmund realised he was still babbling. "Yes, by all means. Er, do you know anywhere?" He looked up the street one way, then the other. All he could see was shacks, one after the other, each one a different size and shape, but nothing at all resembling a bar or cafe.

"Edmund, it's a wonder you can find your way back to an aircraft carrier. Do you leave a trail of breadcrumbs?"

Edmund was about to protest, but saw Barbara's wry smile. She was toying with him. She looked at her watch. "Three o'clock. The Korner should be open. That's Korner with a K, don't ask me why. Should be able to get a cup of tea anyway. Alright, follow me."

Edmund did as he was told, following as she threaded between knots of civilians milling in every direction and none, tiny naked children dashing and hollering, sailors and soldiers looking as lost as he felt. Before too long they were seated at a rickety table in a sort of courtyard, each with a mug of tea and a slice of surprisingly edible sponge cake in front of them.

"It's one of the better places," Barbara said. "It's one of the only places, but still. Run by the WRVS. Better cake than you get in England these days. They aren't short of eggs, you see."

As if to prove the point, a chicken scuttled by the table, clucking, and a woman stepped out, scooped it up and carried it back as if this were a routine occurrence.

Barbara laughed. "See?"

Edmund couldn't help but smile, but there was still the knot in his middle. The telegram. And now Barbara appeared in person. Had she come to be a witness in his court martial? No, that would take place in England wouldn't it? His mind tumbled. "Look, when I got the telegram, I thought..."

"Yes, I can imagine." She was suddenly serious. "But that's why I had to come out, don't you see? Even though it was a thousand to one chance that I'd actually be able to talk to you. I was angling for Gib at first, but then I heard you'd been transferred to *Indom*, and the word was she'd be putting into Freetown before the... Before sailing. So that seemed like the best place to try and catch up with you."

"Crikey." It was all Edmund could find to say.

"You can say that again."

"So, your father..." Edmund gritted his teeth. Why did

he have to speak before thinking? He dared a quick glance at Barbara. Her face resembled cumulonimbus, slate grey and boiling.

"You think I asked Daddy to pull strings and I just hopped on a boat, is that it?"

"No, I...it...just..." He shrugged and tried to pull his face into a conciliatory expression, whatever that might look like.

Barbara narrowed her eyes, then snorted and burst into laughter. "Oh, Edmund. You can stop gurning. Honestly, I'm beginning to wonder why you ever went out with me."

Edmund had been wondering why he had ever broke up with her, then a picture of Liena rushed into his thoughts and everything became very tangled indeed.

"Well," Barbara went on. "I had to get out here. I simply had to. Pulled every bloody string of my own I could, and then some. As it happens I was becoming rather valued at home. Did I tell you about the wireless course? Turns out I'm pretty good. But if anything, they need people in places like this even more, and I thought it's not fair for the likes of you to have to trawl all over the world and people like me get to stay at home in comfort." She cocked her head and spread her arms, as if showing off her dress for that night's party. "So here I am."

"Yes, here you are. I can still hardly believe it."

"But believe it or not, all that aside, I came out to this blasted hell-hole partly to talk to you, you silly man."

"But I thought- oh."

Barbara frowned. "What did you think?"

"That...that...." He sighed, closed his eyes. How could he

have been such an idiot? "That you'd told your father out of spite, and sent me the telegram to rub my face in it."

Barbara's eyes widened, then narrowed. "Edmund! Did you really think I could be such a...a...*harpy*! Oh goodness. You don't know me at all, do you? I was thinking I'd been such a fool, but I haven't been half as much a fool as you."

Could it be true? "Lord, Barbara. I'm sorry, I didn't mean... I mean, what was I supposed to think?" He pulled out the rumpled slip of paper. "You just said you told D... Your f... The Captain about my...ahem, er, score. And he'd reported it."

Barbara twisted her mouth mulishly. "Well I couldn't very well say '*the A2SL intends to divulge your questionable air-combat claims to the Admiralty*', could I? They'd never have let me send the telegram. And besides." She looked at her shoes. "I didn't have enough money for any more words."

"Ah." Edmund rubbed his face.

"Give it here." She plucked the telegram from his hand, stared at it intently for a moment. "I suppose it does look a little stark, doesn't it?"

"A *little*?" Edmund suppressed a snort. "Why'd you tell him, anyway?"

She raised one eyebrow. "Believe it or not, I was rather upset when I read your letter. Well done for making it very nearly as curt as a telegram, by the way. And Daddy always knows when something's wrong and wheedled it out of me."

"Yes, I suppose he did." Edmund had only met the Captain once. It was enough.

"And once I started talking, I couldn't stop. But before you left, after those pompous newspaper articles, you were so cut up about it all, and I was afraid...well, that you'd do something silly."

"But...but..." Edmund stared. Was this really the same girl he'd known back in England? "But it seemed so important to you. All that business at parties? *This is Edmund, he's very nearly an ace, you know*?"

Barbara leaned back in her chair and gazed at him. Not cumulonimbus this time. Stratus. Icy. Inescapable. "You know," she said softly, almost a whisper amid the bustle around them. "I was rather proud of you. And I wanted you to know how proud of you I was. With all those desk-wallahs in their immaculate uniforms strutting all over London acting as though they were winning the war. And you were up there, my poor boy, being shot at and actually doing something to beat Hitler. And you might not have looked like a model from a Gieves and Hawkes catalogue but I wanted them to know you were better than all of them put together."

"Oh."

"Yes. Oh." She grinned lopsidedly. "I don't think we were ever really on the same frequency, were we?"

Edmund nodded. "I have entirely the wrong set of crystals."

Barbara laughed again at that, and Edmund felt a stab. He'd actually missed that sound and never even realised it. But then perhaps it was better this way. If he hadn't misread Barbara so much, he might never have had the courage to speak to Liena. And he could still sense her, like a magnesium light, across half a continent and a war-torn sea, on a bomb-wrecked island.

Edmund looked up and opened his mouth to speak at the same time as Barbara did the same. "Go on," they said simultaneously. He opened his hand and waved her on.

"There is someone else, isn't there?" Barbara said.

Somehow, with all the steam and heat, Edmund felt his face becoming even hotter. "I...well...not..." He sighed. "When I wrote to you, it was...not exactly. And I still don't know if anything will come of it."

"None of us knows anything much of the future these days, do we? Alright, why don't you tell me about her? It is a *her*, is it? I mean to say, you seemed pretty attached to that big gun you mentioned in your previous letter, the one you were waving about on that destroyer? I assume I haven't been thrown over for a Vickers Gas-Operated or something like that?"

"It was an Oerlikon twenty mil. No, it's..." He felt himself reddening again. "But I... Wouldn't that be...?"

"Edmund." She folded her arms. "Shut up and talk."

He was about to make some excuse, then to find something cursory to say, but in a moment found himself pouring out the story of the time he first met Liena, in the middle of the air raid in Valetta, and then the second time, after a strafing from a Messerschmitt and Godden crashing their car... As he heard the words coming out of his mouth, somehow not quite controlled by the thoughts in his head, he realised all over again the power Liena held over him. A power he had submitted willingly to. Deep, dark brown eyes, shining, her olive skin, and a spirit that seemed to latch onto his soul and fill it with electricity.

It struck him with all the force of a cannon shell at point-blank range, that somehow he had to get back to Malta, sooner or later, and frankly the sooner the better. Who knew how much time he had left? Who knew how long Liena had? Every day more bombs were falling on Malta, and if flying, white-hot shrapnel didn't get you, starvation or typhoid might.

Malta or bust, then.

"Well, well." Barbara whistled. "Look who's been well and truly struck down by Cupid's golden arrow."

"Oh Lord, what on Earth have I been blathering about?" Edmund felt himself flushing again.

"I asked, didn't I?" Barbara's cheery mask was back in place. Her mouth made a momentary moue, but her eyes were smiling. "Don't worry, I always knew you never felt as strongly as that about me. And after hearing that, I oughtn't be satisfied with any chap who doesn't shake me up like your Liena does you, eh?"

He grinned, despite himself. "Don't sell yourself short."

"I'm too busy for all that nonsense anyway. I've decided I'm going to be the first woman admiral."

"I should think it'll take you around six months." They both smiled and Edmund knew that however long they both lived, they would always be friends.

"So it's settled then," Barbara said. "You have to get through your tour and get back to Malta and win your Liena properly."

"We have to save Malta first," Edmund retorted, a little more grimly than he should have. Barbara looked suddenly serious, and he decided the change the subject. "Did you really come all this way just to explain about that telegram?"

"Well. Partly. Mostly. But not entirely." Barbara pursed her lips, looked side to side, leaned forward. "Do be careful, Edmund. Not just in the air. I don't know how it will work out. I know that when Daddy raised it, there were those in the Admiralty who would've liked to see you torn down. The Air Department never liked all that 'ace' business, hated it in fact. They think it's frightfully gauche and want to leave all that to the air force. There was a bit of a to-do. One or two wanted you court-martialled as an example of what can happen when we start lauding individuals over the service as a whole."

"Oh." Edmund felt all the warmth drain from his face. Court-martialled?

"Don't fret. When I left, cooler heads were winning out. With any luck it'll all be water under the bridge before long. But I suggest keeping your head down for a while. Try not to draw any more attention to yourself. And whatever you do, don't give them any more reasons to bring you down, alright?"

Edmund nodded but something about her manner made his stomach lurch. This was serious. His mouth was dry all of a sudden.

"There is one more thing," Barbara said, leaning towards him. "Someone did say something to the newspapers. I think I stopped it, I had a word with a family friend, and he...well, I think it'll be OK."

Edmund felt a lurch. "What do you mean?"

Barbara looked down. "Well-"

"Clyde!" A shout boomed out behind him and Edmund turned to find himself looking up at Brierly, grinning all over his face. He nodded at Barbara and back to Edmund. "Well, you work fast."

Oh Christ, this was the last thing he needed. "Um, I, oh, hello Brierly. Er, this is B- er, Third Officer Thomalin. A good friend from England. Ah, Third Officer Thomalin, this is Lieutenant Brierly. He's from my squadron."

"Delighted," Brierly said. "Wonderful to see a charming young Englishwoman in this pigsty."

"Thank you," Barbara said acidly.

"Sorry though I am to love you and leave you, we have to be getting back to the ship Clyde."

Edmund looked at his watch. "Oh blast, you're right." He turned back to Barbara, desperate to know what she had been about to say, unable to ask with Brierly there. How much trouble was he in? "Lovely to see you. I honestly appreciate...everything."

She stood "My pleasure Edmund. Do pay some mind to what I said, won't you?"

"Of course." They shook hands, stiffly. "Well, until the next time."

"Be careful Edmund."

"I will."

He turned to go before any further awkwardness could ensue and strode away with Brierly trailing in his wake.

"I say!" Brierly said when he'd caught up. "How do you know the commissioned lovely back there?"

"Her father takes a particular interest in my career,"

Edmund replied. "He's a big noise in the Admiralty."

"Ah, friends in high places, eh?"

"Not exactly."

1 August 1942

By the time *Indomitable* had finished replenishing stores and put to sea, the new Hurricane was ready. Edmund inspected it as best he could in the confines of the hangar, ducking below and dodging around wingtips and propeller blades to see every part. The smell of its fresh paint was a tang overlaying the familiar atmosphere of the hangar. Where the new coat had been applied, there was a smoothness, a satin sheen to the Hurricane. The code '6-Z' had been added in large duck-egg characters, and beneath the cockpit, 'Lt E. Clydesdale'. Edmund smiled. Even working at a rush, the maintainers had pride in their work. In their pilots. In him.

He secured clearance for an air test as soon as they were free of the land, got into his flying kit and stretched out on a couch in the aircrew ready room. The carrier shifted beneath his back, its motion evolving from a short pitch in the coastal shallows to a languid sinuousness as it entered the ocean.

He didn't mean to doze but seemingly an instant later, Charlie was shaking him awake. "They're bringing her up, sir," he grinned.

Edmund thanked Charlie, shook his head clear of stupor and stepped out of the crew room onto the flight deck. The breeze was brisk, even a little cold. He let the salt-bite of it pour its vitality into him as it funnelled around the island.

The for'ard lift was whining its way skyward and in a moment, his Hurricane was emerging from the depths, sideways on, manhandled straight by a bustle of deck party, and rolled aft, to where Charlie, with a smaller party, was readying a trolley-accumulator. Unbelievably, after all this time, a twinge of nerves creased his middle, and he smiled at the foolishness of it. Would it ever feel familiar? Commonplace?

But the pre-flight had its own rhythm, and drove trivial thoughts away. He and a couple of maintainers heaved the prop round a few times to work any bubbles out of the hydraulics, push a bit of oil around the engine. The exertion left him sweating, a pleasant ache in his arms and legs. Everything was in order, and he climbed onto the wing root and into the cockpit, glanced up and the goofers' and wished he hadn't. A crowd had already gathered. True, there had been no flying for days and this would be the first excitement since the last exercise. But no doubt most of them just wanted to see if he buggered up the landing again. Or the take-off, this time. He resolved to ignore them.

They got the engine going, and Edmund let it warm up, feeling all the pressures and temperatures building as though the aircraft was an extension of his own body. As the aircraft came to life, a metallic, oil and cordite scent began to permeate the cockpit. He could taste it in his mouth, unique, like every aircraft has its own flavour. This one was all sharp newness and action. He could feel himself settling into it. The Hurricane had accepted him.

Finally he could put it off no longer, and waved that he was ready. Wings gave the signal, the DCO dropped his flag. The hands on the chocks pulled them free. Edmund advanced the throttle, let the brakes off and felt the Hurri pick up its skirts and run.

There was a ribbon of unfamiliarity slicing through the usual Hurricane sensations. The acceleration was different, the balance just a touch outside the normal, response to the controls a hair away from what he was used to, and yet before he'd reached the end of the deck, the aeroplane was feeding him with confidence. It hurled him out over the turquoise waves.

The prop was a Rotol, different to the DH on his old Hurri, better, making things just a touch more responsive. He retracted the undercarriage, slid the canopy closed and set the trim for the climb.

It was true, this machine was a little heavier, but the difference wasn't too noticeable, and the prop was making up for it to an extent. When he levelled out at eight thousand, tested the controls and tried a few manoeuvres – that was when the machine came alive. There was a tightness, a solidity to it that defied the roar of the 300mph wind around it, the Gs loading up the wings. Perhaps just because it was new, but it responded so sharply, precisely, it made his last Hurricane feel woolly. Up and round into a wingover, and he was pointing at the sea, feeling the forces build as the aircraft raced downhill and back onto the level, pointing at the carrier. He let the speed build and carved into a barrel roll, watching the waves crash above his head for a moment, then when the wings were level again, he let the Hurricane continue its dive, back towards *Indomitable*, thundering past the carrier at 200 feet, then pulling up and into a slow roll. First, he felt a sort of lightness spreading through his body, and then a searing pulse of joy.

This was just a test flight of course, and soon he would need to call it a day. It was a shame. Once he had confessed his sins to Haddow, he might not get the chance again for a while. He added a flick roll to the end of the last manoeuvre, and built up speed for a big, lazy loop, turning into the circuit when he'd finished.

Despite himself, he felt his heart begin to judder as he put the Hurricane into its final approach, a tight, banking curve from port to keep the batsman in view until the last moment. That crowd on the goofers' was only going to have grown. They'd all be there, waiting for him to screw up – probably willing him to screw up. But the Hurricane was solid, steady beneath his hands. It conferred its confidence to him, and as Bats signalled slight adjustments – left, left, lower, on track – he knew he was going to get down alright. The curve of the round-down rushed at him, but Bats was signalling OK, OK, and on the Cut! he closed the throttle and the fighter settled onto the deck, a snowflake on a puddle, making barely a bump as the hook pulled the wire.

Edmund felt like standing on his seat and giving a bow to the assembled onlookers, concluded it was best not to tempt fate. Charlie clattered onto the wing-root and helped him with the harness. He was grinning all over his face. "Well sir, how was she?"

"Top hole. Absolutely marvellous." Edmund found himself grinning back. "You've done wonders. How was the show?"

"Bloody good. I think you impressed that lot," the rigger added, tilting his head at the goofers in the gallery. "Bunch of tricoteuses."

Edmund laughed. "They'll have to get their thrills elsewhere."

Perhaps if they hung around outside Lieutenant-Commander Haddow's quarters... Edmund felt the colour drain from his face. No backing down now. He changed out of his flying kit and was about to leave the crew room to see Haddow when the door opened and the head of Bill, Haddow's writer, appeared round it. "CO wants to see you sir, right away if you please," he said and was gone before Edmund could reply.

Damn, what now? It would hardly be to congratulate him on his landing. A dressing down for beating up the carrier perhaps? Edmund felt his insides coiling and uncoiling. Why had he done that? Still, he'd stayed well clear of the ship, and had made sure he had enough height if anything had gone wrong. Blast it, why couldn't he get free of this confounded paranoia?

He squared his shoulders and marched through the passageways aft, until he was standing outside the writer's office, knocking like a schoolboy summoned for the cane.

"Ah, Lieutenant." Haddow looked up from his desk when Edmund had been admitted. "How was the new kite?"

"Just the ticket sir," he said, trying not to let the suspicion show in his voice.

"Good. You were lucky we had a spare."

"I know sir. Maintainers did a splendid job."

"Yes they did." Haddow maintained his gaze for a moment longer, saying nothing. Edmund felt his palms slickening. "Anyway," Haddow added eventually. "I'd like your help with something. In a couple of days we're going to join some other carriers for exercises relating to the upcoming op, and it would be helpful to have your contribution to the details."

"Oh?" So it wasn't to be another dressing down! "I mean, of course sir! Now?" Balls. He could hardly raise the business with the claims and Barbara's father now. He'd have to find another moment. Christ, after having built up to it...

"Yes." Haddow raised an eyebrow. "Unless you had anything better to do?"

"No, of course not sir."

"Alright then. Come in, no need to hover like that."

Was Haddow testing him? No, don't be a fool, this was a perfectly natural thing for a squadron commander to discuss with his senior pilot. He'd better do his best with it. Despite everything, Edmund did not want to give the slightest chance of proving Haddow right about him. Not yet.

Haddow sat on the bed, clearing a space among the spill of papers as he did so, and offered Edmund the chair. As he sat, Edmund caught a glimpse of a framed, colour-tinted photograph perched on a corner of the desk. Haddow, with his arm around a girl, more different than the squadron commander than it would be possible to imagine. She was tiny, with light hair and laughing, green eyes. Younger sister? He quickly looked back to Haddow who had caught him staring.

"Susan. Nurse," he said, in a monotone, as if that answered all questions. "Now, shall we?"

Haddow sketched out the exercises that they would be taking part in – called Operation Berserk, appropriately enough. Someone at the Department of Naval Plans hadn't lost their sense of humour. They'd last for three days, as long as the operation itself. Edmund couldn't stop his jaw dropping open when Haddow told him how many carriers would be involved.

"Five – although one of those is *Argus*, and she's just bringing aircraft to Gib, she won't be taking part in the op itself."

Edmund shut his mouth and nodded slowly. "That's probably for the best. "She was lucky to make it through, last time. Far too slow. Who else have we got?"

"Us, and *Eagle*, obviously. *Victorious* is coming from up north – they've called a halt to the Arctic convoys after that shambles with *Tirpitz*. Then there's *Furious* – she won't be part of the escort though, she's carrying Spitfires to deliver to Malta and won't have any of her own fighters. But we still have to co-ordinate with her."

"Five. Good Lord." Edmund shook his head. How on Earth did you co-ordinate five carriers? Even the Japanese only had four at Pearl Harbour!

Haddow set out the challenges. Just manoeuvring the carriers would present problems, giving them enough room to turn into wind when launching and recovering aircraft, not getting in each others' way, but not covering such a huge area of sea that they would be easily detected. And then there was the question of directing the aircraft from each. With two small carriers during the last convoy, it was easy enough for each to control its own fighters, especially as *Argus* had taken the low-level patrol and *Eagle* the high-level. With five carriers, each with different radar and air groups made up of different aircraft, it was like simultaneously playing several games of chess, in three dimensions. They went through half a dozen schemes, none of which seemed short of problems. Edmund could not help but feel Haddow was unimpressed with his contributions.

"It's got to be flexible," the squadron commander huffed. "We have to be able to switch the air groups around at short notice if need be. As you mentioned about the last show, they went for the carriers first. We might expect the same this time, and we need to act on the basis that one carrier could be knocked out."

Edmund scratched his head. "What if two carriers are knocked out?"

"Then, we're fucked. But we won't need to worry about co-operation any more."

"Oh. I suppose that's true." And if two carriers were knocked out, they'd have more immediate concerns than inter-ship co-operation anyway.

"It'll be tricky," Edmund said. "*Victorious* has all the Fulmars and Martlets, if they get her then that's the low and medium cover gone. We'd have to take Hurricanes from the high cover. They're hardly ideal below ten thousand, and it would thin out the high escort. We might find ourselves stretched too thin everywhere. So if that happens, do we try and cover everywhere? Or forget the medium cover and shore up high and low?"

Haddow shrugged. "Fulmars are useless anyway. The Martlets would be a loss but there's only a handful of them. Still," Haddow looked at him piercingly. "You managed alright during Harpoon with less than half what we've got."

Edmund rubbed his face. There was no way to guarantee success, was there? They'd just have to manage as best they could. "Ah. Well. We lost most of the merchantmen."

"The carriers didn't – all but one were undamaged when the heavy escort withdrew. It was the Crabs on Malta who dropped the ball there." He snorted. "Dozens of Spits and Beaufighters and they couldn't match what the Navy achieved on a handful of clapped out Hurris. Let's hope they don't let us down again, eh?"

Edmund's mind was by now tumbling with recollections from the convoy back in June. He ignored the dig at the RAF. It was not untrue, but having spent a bit of time on Malta, he knew they didn't have it easy. "It's all about the fighter direction," he continued. "Tricky – the director on *Eagle* – was a whizz at positioning us in the right place, usually up-sun. One or two Hurris could break up a formation if they got the interception spot on. And once the bombers got scattered, they had virtually no chance of making a successful attack."

"Hmm." Haddow stroked his chin. He had already

turned his eyes away from Edmund and had fixed his gaze on the charts and lists on the desk. "Anyway. This is what the exercises are intended to tease out. I suggest we boil everything down to three or four ways of arranging the air defence, and we can try 'em out over the next few days. Agreed?"

"That sounds like the best we can do," Edmund replied, trying not to grimace. It wasn't as though he'd added much.

"Alright, we'll leave it there then," Haddow sighed. "We'll just have to hope we don't do more harm tripping over ourselves than the enemy does. Thank you Lieutenant, I'll leave you to get on."

Edmund stood. "Thank you sir."

Haddow nodded cursorily. "Dismissed."

Well, Edmund thought, I will be, soon enough.

5 August 1942

The few days after the discussion with Haddow passed in a blur. There was so much work to do that Edmund barely thought about the mess he'd made of things, and the inevitable bigger mess when he faced up to it. There were pilot pairings to finalise for each section, maintenance schedules to make sure all the Hurricanes were in tip-top condition, and none were caught needing a major service or an engine change on the eve of the convoy.

After all, the convoy would be vital, whether he was on it or not. He had to do whatever he could to help it get through. *Had* to. When he thought back to that bomb-plastered patch of rock in the sea, the twitch-ridden aircrews dragging themselves into the air day in, day out, in aircraft that would be condemned under any other command... And the people. The erks and soldiers and civilians, dear Lord, the civilians, with a quiet resolve like the rock the place was grown from. Scrape away at it, and it merely got stronger. Indomitable. That was the word.

Even resolve like that would fail without food. With a grimace at the recollection, Edmund thought of the rations he'd had to get by on. Twelve ounces of bread, six of tinned meat, plus a tinned sausage on Wednesdays. Three cups of tea. Three! The June convoy had only bought them a couple of months and now they were running on empty again. If Malta was to survive, let alone play a part in the war, this convoy was it. There would be no more chances. So it was up to him to do whatever he could.

Edmund flew with as many of the pilots as possible, trying to build up a sense of their strengths and weaknesses, without putting undue stress on men or machines. By Wednesday of that week, time had run out. The following day they would rendezvous off Gibraltar with the other carriers, and the exercises would begin.

His head spun. It was too much to take in. He needed fresh air. Edmund bolted from the tiny cabin and its tinier desk heaped with paper and headed for the deck. As he ascended to the goofers' Edmund felt the deck shift beneath his feet and grasped a stanchion. The carrier was turning into wind. Brierly was the only person up there. Edmund closed the door behind him and uttered a greeting.

"What's going on down there?" Edmund grimaced and nodded towards the flight deck aft, where deck hands were unrigging the arrester wires. The last thing they needed, today of all days, was for the wires to have worn out! "Problem with the gear?"

Brierly chuckled. "No, not as such. Only that it's in the way."

Edmund's brows creased. "In the way? Of what?"

A smile spread across Brierly's face. "You'll see." He nodded aft.

Edmund leaned over the rail and peered into the blue, an indefinable dread settling in his midriff. There was a light haze over the sea and it was hard to tell where it ended and the sky began, but above that it was clear. After a moment, his eyes snagged on something, more sensed than seen, and he returned to that spot until a biplane unmelted into distinctness. A Swordfish – unmistakeable, even at that distance, when you'd seen as many of them as Edmund had over the years. But something unusual about it... carrying something under the wings? No, that wasn't it. It was a floatplane.

"Can't be for that, it's wearing boots," Edmund said, half to himself. "Why've they taken the wires down?"

"Either someone or something very important is on their way. If the latter, it can't wait a moment. If the former, they really don't like getting their feet wet."

Edmund snorted, "you're having me on."

Brierly just leant back and folded his arms. The Swordfish approached, struggling at full throttle to make ground against the wind. And it just kept coming. Edmund expected it to fly over the flight deck, break to port and land alongside. Instead, it approached, floating lower and lower, down towards the round-down. Just as Edmund was certain the pilot would open up the throttle and climb away, the floatplane sagged towards the deck. He let out an involuntary yelp, and a moment later the floats touched, a brief spray of sparks and within a few feet, the Swordfish had shrieked to a stop. The pilot must've forgotten he had floats and not wheels! Edmund turned to Brierly in disbelief but the other was simply laughing.

"The look on your face. They do it every so often. Doesn't damage the floats at all. Ah, that'll be our Captain's sealed orders."

Two figures were climbing out of the rear cockpit. An officer, by the looks of things, carrying a satchel no doubt stuffed with the latest intel reports and the orders Brierly noted, and another figure who, from the stiff way he was moving, was rather older than the average Navy man. Was there something familiar...?

The officer with the satchel disappeared into the island. A sour taste flooded Edmund's mouth. What if it wasn't sealed orders? What if it was instructions to remove a senior pilot from duties to await a court martial? What if he'd be going back to Gib in that Stringbag, under arrest? His chest felt taut. He realised he was breathing fast. Couldn't seem to get enough air. Come on now, it might be nothing. He turned away from Brierly, affecting to focus on something else, anywhere else, as he dragged a breath in, like a drowning man breaking surface.

The Swordfish. Focus on that. The pilot had not climbed out, or even switched off, and a deck party was moving to the wingtips. Edmund watched, open mouthed, as they cajoled the floatplane, engine blipping to help them, over to the crane at the after end of the island, right below where he stood. The officer, having delivered his package and presumably a swift briefing to the Captain, dashed back out and clambered back into the aft cockpit. At least Edmund would not be dragged away right now. Those papers might still be his court martial though... The Swordfish, look at the Swordfish. No sooner was the pilot seated than the crane began to hoist, and the biplane was swung out over the water churning down the carrier's flank. Edmund held his breath as it lolled in the swilling ocean, the pilot standing in his seat to unhook the slinging gear, and then the floatplane was taxiing through the waves, accelerating in plumes of spray, dancing on the wavetops, and finally, lumbering skyward, water streaming from the floats. The whole episode had taken mere minutes.

Edmund shook his head. It felt unreal. Were the Marines coming for him as he waited? Nothing he could do about it if they were. Christ, it was intolerable. Think about something else. Anything.

He was not on flying duty today but there was paperwork to deal with – there always was now he was senior pilot. He let the breeze swirl around him, imagining it blowing all the anxiety away. It usually worked. Not today.

He could bury himself in his work anyway. There were the sections to organise, and it was important to get those right. Pairing a more experienced lead with a junior who would work well with them in the air. There would be no room, or time, for confusion, for lengthy explanations before or during each sortie, so they'd have to be on the same wavelength. He took out his pocket book and a pencil, and made some trembling adjustments to his draft. Then there were suggestions on fighter direction to consider. It was best to have some form of centralised control, of course, rather than each carrier trying to control her own aircraft as they'd been able to do on Harpoon. There were some lessons from Malta, where everything was integrated. Though why he was bothering was anyone's guess. No doubt as soon as he was discovered, Haddow would tear up anything he'd worked on and start from scratch.

Haddow. Jesus. Imagine the look on the CO's face when he realises he has been proved right.

Once Edmund was moderately content that he had something worth writing down properly and giving to Haddow for approval, or, more probably disapproval, he left the goofers', descended from the island and scurried aft to his cabin. If they were planning to apprehend him, they'd be waiting there, surely.

As he entered the passage where he and 800 Squadron's other officers were accommodated, Edmund glimpsed a figure coming the other way. A Marine? No, thank goodness, looked like a civilian. He flattened himself against the bulkhead to let them pass, looked back – and inhaled sharply. A familiar face was looking back at him.

"Vickery! As I live and breathe!" Edmund grasped the journalist's hand and shook it. "Good Lord, it was *you* on the Stringbag!"

"It was indeed," Vickery replied. "I've just had a brief

interrogation with the Captain and been settled into my cabin – lucky there's no Admiral sailing with us."

"Oh, you have a staff officer's berth do you? No camp bed on the writer's office floor this time! What on Earth are you doing here? No, that's a silly question, your job, obviously. I mean why *Indom*? I'm delighted of course." Edmund made himself shut up. He was babbling. He realised he'd been pumping Vickery's hand for at least fifteen seconds and released it abruptly.

The journalist smiled gently. "My dear Clyde. What I'm doing here at this very minute is trying to find a cup of tea. You wouldn't help an old man in his forlorn quest would you?"

They repaired to the wardroom where Edmund had the steward bring them each a mug, though there would be no more time for anything other than the briefest of reunions before Edmund had to return to work. Vickery! Here! It was almost, but not quite, enough to banish thoughts of his impending court martial for a time. Though as nobody had come to lay a hand on his shoulder in the half hour since the Swordfish had arrived, Edmund dared to begin to hope. Perhaps it was just orders for the operation after all. Most likely that was what it was.

The reunion was hardly sufficient. Since they had last spoken, during the heat of the last convoy, aboard HMS *Eagle*, only a couple of months had passed and yet with everything that had happened, it seemed like years. They had exchanged letters, but he had not been able to give much detail of what he had been doing. Edmund sketched out the wild couple of days after he had landed in the drink after bailing out of his Hurricane – being picked up by HMS *Hindscarth*, taking over at one of their anti-aircraft guns, facing the onslaught of dive bombers, a frenetic battle with Italian cruisers... He skated over what he'd done on Malta. He wasn't sure how much Vickery knew, or was allowed to know. For his part, Vickery had flown back to England, spent some time covering Army Co-operation Command, heard of another do in the Med and wangled his way out again.

"I'm nearing retirement, to tell you the truth," he said with a shake of the head. "But I couldn't miss this one." He drained the end of his tea. "It feels like the most important battle there has been for some time. The result will be far-reaching, I'm sure of it. The fate of the war may rest on it."

Edmund exhaled slowly. "You could be right. People aren't usually aware when they're present as history turns, are they? I'm not sure I like it."

"Oh, don't mind me," Vickery smiled. "No need to look at the mountain you're about to scale – just you concentrate on the next rock."

Edmund noticed the glint in Vickery's eye. "Who gave you that bit of advice? Mallory?"

"No, poor old Sandy Irvine."

"Ha! Oh Lord, you aren't joking. You'll have to tell me about that some time."

"Gladly."

"...But later, unfortunately." Edmund checked his watch. "I must be off. I'm ever so glad to see you though, you can't imagine."

They shook hands and Edmund retreated to his berth. Knowing the journalist was nearby was reassuring in itself. For the first time since he had stepped aboard *Indomitable*, Edmund felt he had a friend nearby.

6 August 1942

Thursday dawned to find *Indomitable* west of Gibraltar in a loping swell coming down the Atlantic. Before daybreak, Edmund and Haddow assembled with the CO and Splot of 880 Squadron in the Fighter Direction Office, finalising last minute details and peering at radar scopes in an effort to understand the controller's task. A sub-lieutenant poked his head through a hatch from the adjoining office, said "they're here, green three-zero." and withdrew.

"Alright!" Haddow clapped his hands together and rubbed them. "Let's have a look what the cat dragged in." They ascended to the flag deck, on the very top of the island next to the mainmast, and gazed to the north. Before long, a smear of smoke broke the horizon, then others. The two groups of ships were closing fast. Within minutes, the profiles of two carriers, the almost-mirror image of *Indomitable* which was *Victorious*, and the bent-backed islandless oddity *Furious,* were discernible in among the cruisers and destroyers. The two squadrons carved onto the same course in a flurry of signal gun salutes and flag-hoists.

"Good Lord. Those battlewagons are *Nelson* and *Rodney*!" exclaimed 880's senior pilot. "Thought they with the Home Fleet."

"They are – were, Dickie," replied Haddow. "Russian convoys have been suspended so they're available."

"Is that so? It's a hell of a risk. Some of them get sunk, they won't be able to do the Russian convoys at all."

"We'd better make sure they don't get sunk then, eh?"

"Easy for you to say."

They laughed, but there was a flatness to it. There was little humour in the work that was to come. "Right." Haddow stretched his arms and straightened his cap. "Flying begins at oh-eight-thirty, so let's get ready."

Edmund felt his palms begin to prickle. He would be flying later in the day, but for most of the morning he'd be wedged into a corner of the Fighter Direction Office next to Haddow, hoping fervently that his plans did not go too badly awry. It promised to be the most difficult few hours since he'd arrived aboard *Indomitable*, and none of them had been too easy.

It didn't help that Lieutenant Walpole, the Air Direction Officer, had the unfortunate habit of pipe-smoking, something he indulged near constantly except when actually speaking to pilots in the air. The office was already developing its own layer of 10/10 cloud just below head-height.

There was time for a quick briefing with the pilots in the crew room before the first flight launched. Edmund affected to ignore the sceptical eyes bombarding him with their glare. They didn't trust him. Well, why should they?

"These exercises are mostly not for us," he announced to a desolate absence of reaction. "They're for the fighter directors on the ships, and the Commanders Flying and squadron COs to sort out procedures for the operation itself. Our job is to fly precisely according to instructions, which should, if all goes to plan, bring us out in a good position to intercept an opposing formation. And then report how it went in the debrief afterwards. Bear with them – they've got half a dozen squadrons to marshal and gen from as many ships to factor in. We are but the pawns on their chessboard. So I ask you not to break from instructions or use your initiative..." It hurt to say that, but the mission, the mission was what mattered. "Not very exciting, I'm afraid. Any questions?"

"So if we see any other bombers, we just, what, ignore them?" Ambrose. A sub-lieutenant like most of them. Barely 20, and slouched, sullenly, in his chair at the back.

"That's precisely it. But make sure you report it in the debrief afterwards. As much detail as you can."

"Doesn't give us much practice for the real thing, does it?"

Edmund could hardly disagree, and his pilot's sensibilities were also chafing at the lack of proper practice. But logically, he knew this was the right way. He mumbled something about the importance of getting the direction right, and threw in a vague suggestion they could fit in some mock dogfighting after the exercises. He dismissed the squadron and spent thirty seconds agonising over whether to change the roster so Ambrose was flying as his number 2. No, no, see how today goes. He could always rearrange afterwards if anyone decided they knew better than Admiral Syfret.

The first flights took off, and within ten or fifteen

minutes, Edmund had lost track of what was happening in the skies above. A barrage of communications from aircraft and ships were bouncing around the office, with details from several radar scopes tossed into the mix at seemingly random moments. The ADO and his assistants seemed to be in command of it all, Walpole with his headphones and microphone, his eyes seemingly everywhere. A couple of ratings with chalk and chinagraph pencils constantly scrawled and adjusted points, lines, figures on the blackboards on the bulkhead and the plotting table in the centre of the office. The white Formica disc market with concentric and radiating lines looked like children had been let loose with charcoal. How on Earth could anyone follow what was happening? And on this lay their only hope of breaking the convoy through. On top of it all, Edmund's eyes stung from the smoke and his nose was streaming.

Just when Edmund had managed to reassure himself that no-one other than a specialist could understand the complex dance that was going on around them, something like a cross between football commentary on the wireless and blind-man's buff, Haddow would mutter "*Good, good,*" or "*well that was a blasted shambles!*" Fortunately, just as the first interceptions were taking place, more through the body language of the air direction team than anything else, Edmund was able to pick out the shape of things from the literal and figurative smoke. The interception of two simultaneous dummy raids had been effected successfully. The flow of information from the radar-equipped ships dotted around the fleet had provided the right information at the right time, and more importantly, the operation in place for processing it had proved equal to the task. It was a night-and-day difference to what they had during Harpoon. A lot more potential – but a lot more that could go wrong.

Most importantly, 800 Squadron's pilots had done as they were told. He exhaled as gently as possible. The smoke wafted and tumbled around his head.

Walpole took off his headphones and replaced his pipe. "Well, gentlemen," he directed at Haddow and Edmund. "Any thoughts?"

Fortunately Haddow had enough thoughts for both, and was not shy about volunteering them. As Edmund had surmised, this straightforward task had gone well enough. Other details bobbed to the surface.

"*Victorious'* air warning radar has better high-altitude coverage than ours doesn't it?"

"Mm." Walpole's tone was acid. "And their FDO is a *lot* better equipped."

"It sounds to me as though she should handle the high-level fighters."

"It makes sense, yes, though it pains me to say so."

They carried on the discussion, Edmund contributing little other than to confirm a point or two when Haddow asked. Feeling ever more useless, he began to long for the cockpit of a Hurricane.

Shortly though the discussion was over and Haddow suggested they take a short break. Edmund left the office, heaving in a lungful of cleaner air, and noticed Vickery emerging from the Operations Room at the other end of the passageway.

The reporter nodded a greeting. "Fascinating business."

"You were listening in?" Edmund wondered whether Vickery had followed it any better than he had.

"Yes, what I could understand of it. Didn't have anything like this in 1918. I didn't have much appreciation for the complexities before."

"Let me introduce you to our ADO – that is, Air Direction Officer," Edmund proffered before Vickery could ask any questions he didn't have answers to. "He'll be able to fill you in properly."

Edmund expected Walpole to put up a fight, at least about letting Vickery into the FDO – much of what was in there, the radar in particular, was about as classified as you could get. After the introductions, though, Walpole seemed delighted.

"Charmed," drawled the ADO as they shook hands. "We direct, apparently, because if we attempted to *control* our pilots, it might overcome their delicate sensibilities."

"I see." A small frown momentarily crossed Vickery's face. "Forgive me Lieutenant, do you mind if I ask what you did before the Navy? You look rather familiar."

Walpole beamed, and bowed. "A man of taste, finally, in this overgrown sardine can! *Wise Tomorrow* at the Lyric, perhaps? *The Melody That Got Lost* at Drury Lane?"

An actor? Well, that explained a lot.

"Perhaps," Vickery replied. "Have you done film as well? I recall something with an angel cast out of heaven. Based on a Tolstoy?"

"*What Men Live By*! Goodness, you must've been one of

the seven people who saw it."

"It was a remarkable piece of work," Vickery said – Edmund could not but marvel at the journalist's command of the language. "But, if you'll forgive me, how does one go from the West End to a Royal Navy aircraft carrier?"

"Somewhat easily, it turns out." Walpole leaned forward a touch, as if about to disclose a great secret. "*Enunciation*, you see. The Navy rather likes actors for fighter direction. We bring clarity, precision, and authority."

The perfect job for someone fond of the sound of their own voice... Edmund felt a stab of guilt for his uncharitable reaction but there was no doubting Walpole was in his element. Vickery asked another question and began jotting on a notebook as Walpole spoke. Edmund's attention wandered to the blackboards, showing wind direction and speed, times of sunrise and sundown and the various twilights, and that plotting board with its scatter of marks and scribbles in numerous colours, as though if he stared long enough, the mystery would unveil itself. Before he realised how much time had passed, Edmund realised that Vickery was being ushered out and the preparations made for the next groups to fly off.

This time, the fleet would attempt to manage interceptions at different altitudes. This would be crucial. The enemy was bound to throw a low-level attack by torpedo planes in at the same time as high-level bombers came over. What followed was almost as impenetrable as before to Edmund, but Walpole and Haddow seemed to be gleaning plenty of lessons from it. Edmund resolved, assuming he got through the next week alive, and was not sent home in disgrace, to spend more time figuring out the process. If Walpole let him sit in, he'd surely get the hang of it.

If, if... It was a forlorn thought. He shoved it away.

After the second round the fleet paused for lunch. Afterwards, thank goodness, Edmund was due to fly. It seemed that nothing dampened anxiety around flying better than the alternative, being stuck in a cupboard with the CO and a pipe smoker for three hours. That it was another opportunity to fly his new machine certainly helped. Still, scratching at the back of his mind was the sense that Haddow would be watching his every move, as if he could see into his mind via the invisible waves of the air warning radar. Edmund shuddered. It was a silly notion, pathetic. But he could not shake it off.

Still, it was a relief when he finally took off, leading a flight of four Hurricanes. It was, as he'd told the other pilots, a relatively straightforward business, following the ADO's directions to the letter.

And then, a sudden change of wind direction and strength and he and the others were miles out of position, stuck in a distant stern chase of *Victorious*' Albacores, while the ADO snapped and cajoled. Balls! There was nothing he could have done, but would Haddow understand that? And would his pilots, who had all heard the annoyance in the ADO's voice, haranguing him in front of everyone? They got there in the end and, he reminded himself, part of the purpose of the exercise was to pick up problems like this... But he could still not drive away the sense that it was his own fault. That he was simply destined to fail.

The debrief was excruciating. Edmund's skin prickled and fizzed as he described the sortie. Felt Haddow's gaze spearing into him as he reported the wind shift that had blown the interception apart. *Blaming the weather again are we*, Clydesdale? But the CO said nothing. The atmosphere in the crew room felt closer than it had in the FDO. Harder to breathe. The relief when all was done and they spilled onto the flight deck was explosive. The sea was the green of old copper, glittering painfully, and the salt in the air cut through the fug in his brain.

Vickery was where Edmund expected him to be, on the goofers', watching over all with an aspect of rapt delight. He noticed Edmund after a moment. "Ah, are you all done? I was about to get a cup of tea. Care to join me?"

"It'd be my pleasure! We could get one in the Wardroom." The Wardroom, with all the officers, and Haddow... Why had he said that? "Oh but balls to that. NAAFI canteen alright?"

"Perfect. Lay on, Macduff."

Edmund led them down ladders and along passages, past workshops, cabins, offices, and after only a couple of wrong turns, to the canteen. It was busy, bustling with ratings so after Edmund had procured two mugs of strong tea, they made their way aft and emerged into the open walkway at the quarterdeck, where they leaned on the railing and sipped their tea.

"Quite a nice spot," Vickery nodded approvingly. "One might be on an Atlantic liner."

"You should try it at 28 knots," Edmund replied. "The

shafts are directly beneath us. It's like being a pea in a whistle."

"Ah. Not like the *Queen Mary* then."

"Not so much."

"It was awfully noisy in the canteen," Vickery went on. "Where exactly were we? I lost my bearings completely."

"Somewhat aft of midships," Edmund said, pleased to talk about nothing of importance for a while. "Directly under the lower hangar, just for'ard of the after lift."

"Ah, I think I understand." Vickery nodded slowly. "So most of the racket was coming from the hangar. I thought it sounded a bit industrial for a kitchen. She's a much bigger ship than *Eagle*, isn't she? I didn't quite credit how much bigger."

"You can say that again," Edmund smiled. "I still get lost now and then. Although speaking of finding things, I have to ask – did you happen to know I was on *Indomitable*?"

Vickery met his eye for a moment. "To answer that would be betraying a source, given that the Gazette has not yet listed your new appointment."

Edmund laughed. "I thought I was the one who had to be careful about operational security. Honestly though, it is good to see you."

"You too my boy, you too. I admit I was worried for you on Malta. I heard about... Ahem." He smiled conspiratorially. "Well, sources told me about a rather hair-raising operation over Sicily. But I'm sure you couldn't say anything about that. Tell me, have you had a chance to write anything new recently?"

"Not much." Edmund twisted his mouth. "There doesn't

seem to be much time for poetry."

"I quite understand. But your Valetta Sonnets were splendid, I must say."

"Ah, well." He felt his face reddening. "I don't know. I sent a couple to *Horizon*. Haven't heard anything back yet."

"Glad to hear it. I'd be amazed if they didn't print them. You should send them the lot."

"Oh, I wouldn't want to overburden the editors..." Edmund set his gaze beyond *Indomitable*'s wake, at the warships and merchantmen lurching and bulling through the swell. Poetry felt a long way from this steel citadel, this floating aerodrome. At least, not the kind of poetry he'd found himself drawn to. The poetry of this ship would be something harsh and mechanistic. He could not yet see through to its heart. And poetry required truth. Something he did not have much of at the moment. "Anyway, you'd rather hear about the exercises I imagine."

"In due course," Vickery said, the words pregnant. "I'm not interviewing you at the moment, am I?"

"No, no. Sorry." Edmund sagged into silence once more.

At his elbow, Vickery coughed softly. "I hope you don't mind my asking. But there's something wrong, isn't there? You've seemed preoccupied since I came aboard."

Edmund took a breath, ready to deny it, to breezily insist that everything was fine, it was just that being Senior Pilot was a big responsibility. And he knew Vickery would not push any more if he did that. But the journalist was giving him a chance. To unburden himself, to tell the truth to someone at least, to let some of the sin out for a moment.

Before he could stop himself, he was rattling through the whole story. Vickery knew about the four kills he'd been awarded but not deserved, of course – he was the first person Edmund had told about it. Properly told about it, not blathered something incoherent about cheating, as he had done, half-cut, with Barbara that time. In a minute or two, barely pausing for breath, Edmund had poured it all out. His impulsive confession to the girl, it being passed on to the Admiralty, then to the press, his suspicion that it had got him kicked out of his last squadron – even if that had led to a promotion of sorts – and was probably about to get him kicked out of this one. How Haddow seemed to know of his shortcomings, and was running out of patience. How had it all got so messy?

Vickery knitted his fingers and leaned his elbows on the rail. He remained silent for so long that Edmund began to wonder if the journalist had no idea what to say in response to his outburst, that he'd just made another huge mistake. "You feel you have been dishonest," Vickery said eventually. "More than that, you feel you have benefited materially from this dishonesty. So, you are punishing yourself to compensate for this benefit."

Edmund took a breath to speak but Vickery held up a finger.

"But ask yourself. Is the punishment commensurate with the benefit? Did you even want the benefit? Do you still benefit? It seems to me not. And yet you continue to punish yourself. Tell me, do you really care about...how did you put it before? 'Cricket scores' I think you said. The number of," he paused, and placed the next word as if it were something delicate, or dangerous, "*kills*. Hmm. Let's say 'enemy aircraft destroyed,' just for our purposes."

"No, I don't, not in the slightest." Edmund shook his head as if to tear the idea loose. "I mean, well, it shows you're, I don't know, getting on with things. Not swinging the lead. Not entirely useless. But in themselves..." He shuddered.

Vickery met his eye, then looked back out to sea. "You alluded to some success when you took over that gun on the destroyer?"

Well, there was that. He could be proud of that, at least. Couldn't he? He shrugged. "They fished me out of the water, and were short a gunner. I could operate the cannon so I pitched in."

"But you shot down some aircraft?"

Edmund felt his face colouring. "My ammo-loader thought I got a few. I'm not sure I believe him."

"And on Malta. I understand the raid on Gela destroyed quite a few aeroplanes?"

"That's different, they were on the ground. Oh! How did you know about that?"

The corner of Vickery's mouth tweaked for a second. "I won't tell, don't worry. But they were, on the ground. You got them before they'd even had a chance to menace Malta."

Edmund looked skyward and chuckled. "What's your point? I know you Vickery, you're driving towards an objective like Montgomery."

The journalist smiled broadly. "Merely this. You're worrying about your contribution. I would argue that your contribution does not begin and end at the four victories, whether you feel they do or not. And if you aren't convinced, perhaps that's something to put aside until a quieter moment anyway."

"That makes perfect sense of course." Edmund sighed. "But then when I heard it might have got out. And if some editor does get hold of it, I'm sure they'd print it, even if they didn't name me. I don't care about me, it'll make the Fleet Air Arm look bad, and goodness knows we get little enough support compared to the air force. I don't know how I could look these men in the eye again if it does get out."

Vickery was silent for some moments. "Well," he said eventually, dragging the words out by their roots. "You needn't worry about that."

"I'll try not to of course, but the consequences..."

"No." Vickery was visibly struggling. "I mean there will be no consequences. The story won't get out. Trust me. It's been spiked."

"Spiked? But how... How do you know? What- Oh!" He sat back. There was a tightness across his brow, and he rubbed at it for a moment. If Vickery knew, that meant...

"You're acquainted with Barbara Thomalin, I gather?" Vickery said.

Edmund grimaced. It was all he could do not to slap himself on the forehead. "Of course. She mentioned something about a family friend? That would be you?"

Vickery performed a mock bow. "I've known Captain T since the last war and Barbara since she was born. She came to me, reluctantly – I have the impression she likes to fix her own mistakes if she can. There is, of course, not an editor on Fleet Street I haven't worked with for years, and though I'm not sure many of them like me, for some reason they respect me. I don't believe there was a serious chance of it getting into print, not really, but I prevailed upon the chap who had it to drop it."

"You did that for me?" Edmund felt the blood draining from his face. "Oh God."

"I did it because it was the right thing to do. Even though," Vickery forced a smile, though his eyes remained hard, "I have never got in the way of a journalist reporting a story before and I hope I will never have to again." He sighed. "I don't actually think it was a story, not that that was my decision to make. But I suppose justice has been served, one way or another."

Vickery began to blur. Edmund blinked. "I'm so sorry," he said, his voice sounding distant somehow. "To drag you into this."

"Now I do believe you're punishing yourself again," Vickery replied, with a chastising tone that Edmund recognised as not entirely lighthearted.

Well, it was true wasn't it? If it weren't for all his confounded self-pity, none of this would have happened. He couldn't blame Barbara for a moment's weakness, nor could he really blame Captain Thomalin for dropping him in the soup. Thanks to the consequences of his blasted self-flagellation, Vickery had felt compelled to surrender his principles. Edmund had messed things up alright – just not in the way he'd thought.

"I do believe there is a lesson here," Vickery murmured,

breaking in on Edmund's thoughts. "I hope you'll take the right one."

"Which is?"

"Trust your instinct in the heat of the moment, and afterwards, trust that you were acting in good faith."

Edmund exhaled. He was right. Vickery was right, of course. And having unburdened to him, it seemed easier to do so with Haddow now. He would still have to inform the CO of course. Things were clearer now. He had failed less over the matter of his claims than in letting it take over his thoughts, and in his ill-advised confession that could embarrass the entire Fleet Air Arm. If only he could have trusted himself a bit more.

Vickery stepped back from the rail, and placed a hand on Edmund's shoulder. "It's a grave responsibility you have, you and your comrades, and you're all so young. Don't be so hard on yourself. That's what the enemy is here for. Now, I have a hankering to see more of this ship. Would you show me?"

"Yes. Yes, of course. And thank you, Vickery. I owe you more than a mug of tea, that's for certain."

"You don't owe me anything, my boy. Although I hope you'll consider it the right thing to do to give me a lengthy, detailed and honest interview about this fascinating operation."

Edmund laughed, the relief flooding out as he did so. "You're on."

9 August 1942

After waving goodbye to *Argus* in the early morning of

the 8th as the old ship lurched back up into the Atlantic, the remaining carriers turned east and passed through the Strait of Gibraltar. They spent the day under the Rock, refuelling. Edmund felt conspicuous. Surely there were observers on the Spanish side who would be reporting the arrival of four carriers, three of which were not usually based in the Mediterranean. If it was up to him, they would have oiled at sea and snuck through the straits at night.

"It'd take too long," Haddow snapped when he raised the question just before the pilots' briefing. "Too vulnerable to U-boats, off Gib. The merchantmen have to leave the Clyde with enough fuel for the return journey as well – Malta has none to spare. They know if a torpedo gets them, all that fuel will go up, and... Well, just be glad you're on a thirty-thousand ton armoured carrier and not a floating Molotov Cocktail, eh?

"Ah, I see," Edmund nodded. "I suppose they don't necessarily know where we're going."

"There'll be decoy ops in the Eastern Med, and rumours put about that we're invading North Africa," Haddow added. "Anyway, I wanted to give you a bit of advance notice, as much as possible anyway. All-squadron briefing at oh-nine-hundred. Be there early."

Edmund did as he was told and arrived at the crew room in time to take a front seat. He took a look around as the room filled. Eager sprogs, keen to get their first taste of combat. Old stagers knowing exactly what they were in for and none too happy about it. He cast his eye about, as inconspicuously as possible, trying to spot if any showed signs of incipient 'twitch', anyone relying a little too heavily on alcohol to get them through each sortie. He couldn't see anything like that, but then he'd never been any good at reading people. Then again, Barnes, one of the few old hands, looked a little pale and was pressing his left temple with two fingers. He'd been suffering from migraines, apparently, though it hadn't stopped him flying yet.

The door opened and Edmund noticed Vickery slipping in. He stood to one side at the back, nodding to Edmund, who smiled and nodded back. Damned irregular for a journo to sit in on a briefing but Wings had probably been worked on.

Haddow made his way in, nodded perfunctorily at Edmund, and took a seat. A moment later, the Commander Flying and Intelligence Officer entered. The ready room quietened.

"Alright everyone, this is it," Wings declared. All the captains of the ships in the fleet and the convoy are opening their sealed orders about now, so I can finally confirm what we've been training for these last few weeks, and which will come as little surprise to you. Convoy WS 21S to Malta." He waited as a burst of muttering rippled through the pilots, then died down.

"This has two parts – Operation Bellows, which will deliver Spitfires to the island, and Operation Pedestal, a supply convoy. You'll be aware that we ran a supply convoy through back in June, but only a couple of ships got through. It was enough to keep 'em going for a while, but now it's make or break time. It is imperative that we properly supply Malta with food, fuel and ammunition, enough to last them months and to put the island back on an offensive position. We lose Malta, and the whole of the Med could go like a house of cards."

Edmund felt his pulse quicken. He knew all this very well, but now it meant something real. Liena, simply getting enough food to survive. The pilots and maintainers at Hal Far, eking out the few drops of petrol they had left... Wings went through the details for the next couple of days. R/T frequencies, call signs, air-sea rescue arrangements... Then the most important bit. How the hell it would all work.

"Pay attention to this, because it's important. It's the reason you're all going to be flying so many sorties." Wings left a gap to make sure he had everyone's undivided attention. Edmund hoped no-one else could hear his heartbeat. "During daylight hours on days two and three, there will be a standing patrol of eighteen aircraft."

Edmund whistled. On Harpoon they'd only managed a standing patrol of two! Wings shot him a look, and he hunched lower in his seat.

"...These will be stacked at low, medium and high altitudes. The low patrol will consist of Fulmars. Martlets will take the medium patrol – they have a slightly lower ceiling than the Hurricane but a better climb rate, plus they dive like a brick, so they will be available to help where most needed. Hurricanes will form the high patrol, to catch level bombers, hopefully with enough spare altitude to dive on them. We will also have a stand-by section waiting on deck, which will also be eighteen machines."

It was going to take some choreography not to have them

all tripping over each other. Even after the exercises helped them hone their preparations, the margin between smooth operation and catastrophe was fine.

"...So what about the opposition? We think the Italians have about four hundred aeroplanes at their disposal, the Germans perhaps four hundred and fifty. Only the Italians have torpedo bombers, around a hundred of 'em, but they'll be very much in evidence, along with fifty or sixty level bombers. Other than around fifty Junkers 88s, most of the Jerry crates are Stukas. We won't see them until the third day, what with their range."

"What about fighters?" someone shouted.

"They won't be in range until Wednesday afternoon – fifteen hundred at the absolute earliest, so no need to worry about them too much for now. Our best gen says they have two to three hundred, between the Jerries and the Eyeties."

Edmund felt a hush settle on the room. The fighters alone outnumbered them by two or three to one!

Wings wrapped up, and Haddow stood.

"Alright, make sure you've familiarised yourself with the details Wings has just set out. We only get one shot at this, so no screw-ups." Was it Edmund's imagination or had Haddow just shot a glance at him when he said that? "Now. We're still going to be heavily outnumbered even though we have more aircraft and pilots than any previous convoy. We expect raids will start at some point tomorrow if not this evening, and will go on throughout Wednesday. That will be the big day. All of you will go up twice – some of you, three times. That's why safeguarding crates and pilots is of the utmost importance. No foolish risks, no glory hunting..."

Edmund wondered if he pulled his arms in any tighter, if he'd be able to slip through a gap in the chair and perhaps sink into the lino. He fought to remain immobile, impassive.

"We've all seen pilots getting themselves so intent on a target that they don't see the fellow that shoots them down," Haddow went on, his tone softening a touch. "The worst thing you can do is take yourself and your aeroplane off the field of play by getting shot down or killed. The next worst thing you can do is allow yourself to be pulled away from the convoy chasing a potential kill. You've got about fifteen seconds' worth of ammo. Don't waste it. Your guns are all harmonised on the Admiralty pattern. That means you can fire effectively from five hundred yards. Trying to get in closer than that will not improve your chances of a hit, but it will make you much more vulnerable to return fire. If I hear any of you have been prevailing upon your armourers to change to a point-harmonisation you will be off flying duties immediately. We've plenty of evidence that the Admiralty pattern works. I suggest you trust it."

Haddow stopped to let that sink in. He was right, counter-intuitive though it sounded. However frosty Haddow was towards him, there was no doubting the CO had his pilots' best interests at heart.

"Lieutenant Clydesdale flew in the last show like this one," Haddow went on. What? Oh bloody hell, what now? "...And it's important we take advantage of that experience. Clyde, anything you'd like to add?"

Jesus, it would have been nice if Haddow had warned him he was going to do this. Never mind.

"Ah, er, yes. Well." He stood, looked over the gathered airmen, and could not avoid gulping. "Well. As you'll have heard, we will be well outnumbered by enemy aircraft, but that was the case, even more so in fact, during operation Harpoon. And we were just as undergunned. But when we handed the convoy off to the RAF, we'd only lost one merchantman. We found that it didn't take great numbers of aircraft to succeed, as long as we stuck to the job. Focussed on breaking up the formations, even just forcing them to miss, rather than shooting down aircraft..."

Edmund felt the heat blooming in his ears as he said this last. He'd allowed himself to fixate on a Re2001, after all, pursued it until he ran out of fuel. Wasted a perfectly good Hurricane and taken a pilot out of the line. Idiot.

"Er... So, follow the ADO's guidance. Don't get drawn away from the convoy – for your own sake as much as the convoy's, if you have to ditch, you don't want to be miles away from any ships. Oh, and don't make a direct stern attack on a Junkers, it's suicide. Beam and quarter attacks are much safer. That's all."

He sat, glad that was over. Haddow didn't seem to be displeased, anyway.

"Any questions?" Wings asked.

"*Is it true they put a hole in every tenth johnny?*" someone muttered near the back of the room, to a mix of titters and groans from the others.

"I should think you're living proof of that, Brierly," Haddow snapped.

"...About the operation!" Wings stormed.

Everything had been about fighters so far. In fact, the torpedo boys weren't even in the room. Edmund cleared his throat. "Er, last time there was a sortie by the Italian cruisers. Are there any arrangements for a torpedo strike if that happens again?"

"That was after the carriers parted company, I believe. And they did not press their advantage." Wings looked uncomfortable, suddenly. He seemed to be looking for the words when Haddow stood again.

"We need every fighter in the air as much as possible, so there's no room for Albacores. They'll be struck down at the back of the hangar. The crews have been told off to man the ship's guns, and God knows they ought to be a bit better at aircraft recognition than the usual lot."

A laugh broke out among the assembled pilots, but Edmund inhaled despite himself. That was a gamble. If the battleships came out...it didn't bear thinking about. They'd better hope it was only aircraft they faced. They would be challenge enough.

10 August 1942

Monday dawned. Everyone was tense. Edmund woke as the first muddy glints of light lifted the night. After his experience during Operation Harpoon, he climbed the ladders sunward half expecting the smoke of the Italian fleet on the eastern horizon to greet him. Instead, the sun rose on fog swaddling the convoy. The ships pressed east beneath its obliterating coat. It couldn't last. It would not. By 0500 it was clearing. Twenty five minutes later, the first alert.

The duty section scrambled. Pilots gathered on the goofers' and the quarterdeck, waiting for news. Edmund could see the tension lining the others' faces. He'd been through it a couple of months ago – few of these chaps had. If anything, the knowledge only added to his apprehension. Just breathe, he told himself. There's nothing you can do yet. There'll be plenty to do about it soon enough.

The tannoy crackled and hands tightened on railings all around the ship. "D'ye hear there. Duty section returning," the speakers announced. "Contact was an RAF Sunderland from Gib."

Edmund let his breath out, and heard half a dozen others doing the same. The uncanny peace went on. They were waiting. They must be. The subs and E-boats and torpedo bombers... All waiting to spring an ambush. It was a stretch for aircraft, sure, but not for the U-boats, or the Regia Marina. There should be shadowers by now. Long-range aircraft locating the ships and reporting their position. Imperative to keep them at bay for as long as possible. The further the convoy got, the better its chances.

Another alert – and another false alarm. A Hudson with a malfunctioning IFF beacon, so it looked like a bogey on the radar plot.

The duty sections changed over, and changed again without any further alerts. The day wore on, through the afternoon and into the first dog watch. Finally it was Red Section's turn. Edmund's new Hurricane was brought up from the hangar and lined up aft. He took his seat in the cockpit, went through his checks, and tried to relax.

Wherever he let his mind wander to just seemed to make things worse. He was sweating into his shirt and his palms needed wiping so often his shorts were soaked. The clock ticked round toward 1700.

Then the klaxons blared out across the flight deck, *Fighters, stand to!* Even though Edmund had been expecting it at any moment, he started at the sound. He'd thought he would have got used to this by now, but every time he launched it was as though he'd forgotten how to fly. How to fight.

The deck leaned as the helm went hard over, turning the carrier into wind. Wings was frantically waving from the bridge. Edmund pushed the starter and his Merlin crashed into life. Seconds later, the Hurricane was rolling-floating-bouncing along the deck and climbing away before it had fully passed the island. He glanced in the mirror, noted with satisfaction that Ambrose had got away smartly and was close on his tail. *Indomitable* was already turning to resume her station.

"Single contact, approximately five thousand feet, heading south at just over one hundred knots," *Victorious'* ADO informed them when the pair were airborne. "It'll cross our course in the next fifteen minutes. Steer zero-seven-two and make angels five-five."

They were up-sun at least. Just as Edmund spotted a dark point moving across their course, his radio fizzed. Ambrose. "Contact Red Leader, one o'clock low, crossing to starboard. Looks like a flying boat."

"I see it," he replied, tracking the bogey and altering

course to intercept. It was big, that was evident even at this range. A Catalina perhaps? They were behind now but overhauling it. Two engines? No, four. And the wing was high, but he could see daylight between it and the hull.

Edmund exhaled. Probably Allied. But then it could be Italian, at a stretch, or French. "It's not a Sunderland, Red Two. Can you get a clear ID?"

"Sorry Red Leader. Can't make it out yet."

The Hurricanes drew closer. It looked rather like those big American flying boats that did the transatlantic run before the war. It was certainly that size. A parasol wing, four engines... Looked like radials. Not a CANT anyway, too many engines. He thumbed the radio, "I think it's French. Probably not military, but hard to say from here. Let's get a bit nearer and see if we can see guns."

Edmund felt his heart thumping harder. Any moment, streams of tracer might pour out of the big aircraft. But it wasn't making any effort to evade them. As far as he could tell it was maintaining the same course it had been on when they sighted it, roughly south-south-west.

Ah, there it was. "It's French," he reported. "Civilian. Large, four-engine flying boat. Registration Fox Ack Robert Edward Johnnie."

"Understood, Red Leader," replied the ADO. "He's on an intercept course for the convoy. Try to direct him to the eastward."

Edmund edged the Hurricane closer, gently. If the pilot had any sense he'd try to open the distance and swing east. Good Lord, the aircraft was huge. Hard to judge how close. The vast wing was hanging overhead like a beetling rock. He could hear the rumble of the engines over the sound of his own. God no. Too easy to tangle in those struts. He eased the throttle open for a moment and then again, not letting his eyes break away from the fuselage next to him as the Hurricane gradually began to overtake the flying boat.

Even with him sitting this close, the pilot had not altered course, not a single degree. Damn him, was he trying to crash them both?

Edmund kept easing the Hurricane forward until he judged he was marginally ahead of the flying boat. At this distance it must look as though the Hurricane was trying to park inside the cockpit. He tweaked the spade grip, putting just a touch of left bank on until the fighter was drifting in towards the airliner. For a moment he thought the pilot was finally going to turn. His port wingtip must have been less than 50 feet from the flying boat when it became clear that the pilot was calling his bluff. He sheered away, snarling in frustration.

"No go. The bastard's not deviating."

"Estimate he'll be within visual range of the fleet in less than five minutes, Red Leader," the controller replied. Even with the hiss and scrape of the radio, there was an edge to his voice. "If he's going to sight it, you're authorised to fire on him."

"Understood." Damn, damn, damn. "Alright Red Two, I'm going to give him a warning shot across the bows. Keep well clear, alright?"

"Understood Red Leader," Ambrose replied.

Edmund banked right and opened the throttle to

maximum cruise, S-turning back towards the flying boat on a collision course. At 150 yards, he nudged the rudder to ensure he would pass well ahead, and thumbed the gun button, a good long burst. Tracers sliced across the sky, slashing across the nose of the flying boat. Far enough ahead to be safe, Edmund noted with satisfaction, but close enough to give the pilot a scare. He banked hard and turned away to take up station to starboard again.

Nothing. It was as though the pilot were completely insensible. The flying boat droned on, not having deviated from its course by a single degree.

"Just fired a warning burst across his bows," Edmund told *Indomitable*. "No response."

"Three minutes Red Leader."

"Understood. I'm going to give it one last try." Edmund closed right up on the flying boat's cockpit, as close as he dared. He could see the pilot plainly now, under the greenhouse canopy. The man was trying to look fixedly ahead. Edmund thumbed the gun button briefly. The guns rattled out no more than a half dozen rounds each, but the flying boat pilot's head snapped towards him. They locked eyes. Edmund's palms were slick, and he hardly dared lift one hand off the spade grip to gesture to the pilot. Hand flat, he jabbed it to the left, towards Sardinia. Deliberate motions so there could be no doubt. Turn to port. The pilot regarded him for a moment, then turned away, staring forwards again. In the fuselage windows, white faces regarded him. He could see their apprehension even at this distance. His stomach twisted. Passengers. They must be. Too many for crew.

"Blast it!" Edmund almost growled with frustration. "Stay in touch with *Indom*, Red Two, I'm going to try and find his frequency. At this range he ought to blow my eardrums out."

"Alright. But you'd better be quick." Even through the crackle of the wireless, Ambrose's disapproval was clear.

Edmund had no idea what channel the flying boat might be using, but he worked through the frequencies, forcing himself to go gradually so as not to miss anything. A few that were distant, one clearly scrambled, another that might have been Malta. And then, deafening in his headphones, rapid-fire French, in the clear. He tried to follow it, and had almost given up when the words "*Je suis intercepté par deux avions anglais!*" leapt out. This was it!

"Attention Avion Francais!" he started. Hadn't spoken French in years. "Arrête... no, not stop... Changez votre direction...tournez-vous à l'est. A... un...neuf... zéro. Compres...comprend... Oh, bugger. Do you understand? Un! neuf! Zéro! À l'est!"

The radio operator just kept talking, repeating the same message over and over. It included what sounded suspiciously like a position. He switched frequencies back.

"They seem pretty determined Red Leader," Ambrose said. "I think they might be on a reconnaissance sortie."

"I doubt that, there're passengers on board," Edmund replied. "I don't know what the pilot's playing at. Damn him to hell! I won't shoot down civilians." He fiddled with the R/T again, moving it back to the French frequency. "Listen, for God's sake French airliner, this is the Hurricane on your starboard bow. You MUST alter course to the east or we will shoot you down. Do you understand? If you do not alter course we will have no choice but to shoot you down. Please acknowledge."

The French wireless operator gave no sign of having heard him, let alone understood. He glanced at Red Two. Ambrose was jabbing his finger ahead. Bloody hell. Smoke. A dozen dark smudges could be seen poking above the horizon. Last chance. Edmund edged the Hurricane closer, closer, until it seemed inevitable that the wing would impact on the hull, and pushed the stick forward at the last moment, dragging a ragged breath into his lungs as the Hurri dipped below the airliner. The ships were clearly visible now. It was too late. He reached out to switch the R/T back, just as he heard "...*Deux cuirassés, deux porte-avions, deux croiseurs, quatorze contre-torpilleurs, et douze navire de commerce...*"

Bollocks.

The flying boat pushed on, its course as ruler straight as before. In a minute they were over the convoy, a grid of wakes scoring the surface below.

Edmund's fingers tightened on the spade grip. He flicked to transmit, his voice sounding distant in his own ears. "Sorry Pedestal. They're reporting the convoy. Battleships, carriers and merchantmen. Numbers. And the position. I'm disengaging."

"Understood Red Leader," crackled back through the headphones. "Return to mother."

***

Once he had seen his Hurricane struck down into the hangar, Edmund forced himself to make a marching pace in the direction of Haddow's quarters. He wanted to speak to Vickery. More than anything. To immerse himself in the calm of the journalist's voice, throw himself on the belief that once Vickery spoke, things would make sense.

He dare not. Anything that might stop him, make him back out could not be entertained. This was the time he confessed his fraud to Haddow, mission or no mission, and let fate take its course.

He tapped on the door to the outer office and went in. Haddow's writer was absent, thank heavens. Haddow was seated at his desk. At the door opening, he looked up.

"Sorry to disturb you sir, but I wanted to fill you in on the patrol as soon as possible."

Haddow pursed his lips, put down the paper he'd been reading. "Alright then Lieutenant Clydesdale. Make your report."

"I and Sub-Lieutenant Ambrose were scrambled to investigate a contact approaching the fleet. It was a civilian airliner, sir. I'm not sure of the exact type. A big, four-engine flying boat. It was clearly marked with French civilian ID letters and I could see passengers aboard."

"No need to present yourself as if it were your court martial, Lieutenant."

Yet. Edmund realised he had been standing to attention and addressing his comments to the bulkhead. He relaxed and allowed himself to make eye contact with Haddow. "Er, sorry sir. Despite my best efforts, we were unable to shepherd it away." He rubbed the back of his head for a moment. Had that pilot been on reconnaissance? "We tried everything, both to physically encourage him away, and to communicate with him to that effect. I nearly collided with him more than once. The pilot refused to deviate from his course, speed or altitude."

"And he definitely sighted the fleet?"

"Not only that, but reported it over the radio, more or less accurately."

"On a civilian channel?"

"As far as I know." Edmund shrugged. "He was talking in the clear. Even if the Vichy authorities don't pass on the message, there's every chance the Italians intercepted it anyway."

"Hmm." Haddow scratched his head, his gaze distant. Just as Edmund thought the CO had forgotten he was there, Haddow said: "You were authorised to shoot it down."

It wasn't a question.

"I was." Edmund took a breath. "I know it's not good enough, but I could not shoot down that airliner. I'm aware I've compromised the operation put the lives of the others at risk." And Malta, dear Lord, Malta. What had he done?

Might as well get it all out, before he bottled it again, or the opportunity passed. "I will accept any consequences without complaint, of course. Furthermore, I'm afraid I have, well, something of a confession to make. I wanted to tell you before we got into the fight properly because... Well. Between it and the airliner, I expect you might want to take me off operations. I should have told you earlier. Nobody's responsibility but mine."

Haddow steepled his fingers and gazed at Edmund. He said nothing.

Edmund took a breath. "It's about my four confirmed claims," he said, as levelly and confidently as possible. "Sort of. That is to say, although they were confirmed, I do not believe I am entitled to them, and news of my, uh... that is to say, the possibility of an injustice has come to the attention of certain people at the Admiralty and possibly the press. I thought I ought give you the chance to replace me, but..."

Haddow's face betrayed nothing. After a moment he drawled "Not *much* of a chance, is it?"

"I know sir, Sorry sir. How about Brierly? He's about as senior as I am."

"I tell you what Clydesdale, why don't you pick your own Splot when you have a squadron, eh?"

Edmund choked back a laugh. His own squadron! He'd be going home in disgrace before his feet touched the ground. He feigned a cough, and said nothing.

Haddow raised one eyebrow slightly. "And what do you mean, 'not entitled' to your kills?"

Edmund cleared his throat. "The first simply overshot, flew in front of me. I thumbed the gun button reflexively and he went down. Pure luck. The second happened to stall-in while I was attacking him, don't think I even got a single hit, to be honest. The third I believe collided with my wingman in cloud I foolishly led us into after I had fired on it. The fourth should have been a quarter share, but it was awarded solely to me as flight-leader."

"And that this has... How did you put it?" He struck a pose and put on an exaggerated accent. "*...Come to the attention of divers personages at the Admiralty and the* *press?*"

Edmund reddened, looked at his feet. "I...er...let slip to a girl. And later she got rather upset with me and told her father, who happens to be the Assistant Second Sea Lord. And, to be frank, he didn't like me much as it was. I'm given to understand that it's not likely to result in any action...not from Their Lordships anyway, but the press got hold of it. I'm told they won't print, but..."

Haddow rubbed his eyes for a moment, but said nothing.

"Anyway," Edmund staggered on, "I wanted to inform you so it didn't come as any surprise should it come out. And give you the opportunity to take any action you might want to. To avoid compromising the service."

Haddow closed his eyes and sighed very gently. "Haven't you heard 'careless talk costs lives'? Seen the posters?"

It was basic stuff. "Yes, I have sir."

"'Loose Lips Sink Ships?' What about that? Heard that?"

Edmund felt his face becoming hotter and hotter. "I...yes, sir."

"'Keep Mum, she's not so dumb?'"

"I've heard that one too, sir." Edmund closed his eyes. Lord, he'd spilled his guts to a *journalist* too. Not that Vickery would ever divulge, but still... If Haddow found that out, he'd throw Edmund over the side.

"'The more you keep under your hat, the safer he'll be under his?'"

Edmund frowned. "That does sound somewhat familiar."

"'We could do with girls like you in the Women's Land Army'"

"Yes, yes, I-. Er, what?" Edmund blinked and turned to Haddow.

The squadron commander seemed to be staring. His eyes bulged and his lips pursed oddly. Then he let out a squeak. And then a snort. And then began roaring with laughter, rocking in his chair and slapping the desk repeatedly. "Oh good grief," he wheezed, "is that all? I thought you were going to tell me you'd had your way with Admiral Cunningham's wife or something."

Edmund's mouth fell open, and he shut it with a snap. "Sir?"

Haddow let out another burst of laughter that wound down like a hissing tyre and ended in a sigh. "Is this what's been on your mind the last couple of weeks?"

Edmund nodded.

"Well. Look." Haddow leaned back in his chair. "You should have come to me earlier, but never mind that now. If that's all it is, and honestly it doesn't bother me, then we can put it behind us. All I care about is that the squadron does its job. It's a pretty important job, too, on this show, and we've all got to be our best. Especially you, as Splot. The rest will take their cue from you."

Edmund swallowed. It was a big responsibility, he knew. But he had to be up to it. There was no other way. For Malta... For Liena. He had to be ready.

"But...if it gets out and...embarrasses the Admiralty?"

"Do you think that will make any difference to us, here, over the next couple of days?"

That was a good point, Edmund thought. Let them get through this and then it didn't matter what Their Lordships did to him. He might well be dead within a day or two anyway. A lightness bloomed in his chest at the idea, oddly satisfying, though a tinge of bitter regret crept in after a moment. It was all for Malta, but he might not see it.

"Half our chaps have been relieved and replaced by an almost entirely new lot," Haddow went on. He seemed to be unburdening himself too, now the air was clearer. "It's a good show, I must say – the old guard had been with us a while and everyone starts to feel tired, but as a squadron, we were just about getting into good shape. That's why I need you, Clyde – I can call you Clyde, can't I? – you've been around almost as long as I have. I'll be straight with you – I wasn't happy with your performance over the previous couple of weeks, but I think you know that. Under normal circumstances, I'd have given you longer to find your feet, but I had to push you because we didn't have much time and it's bloody important. I'd heard good things about you so I was confident you'd step up to the mark eventually, I just needed you to hurry up."

"Good things? Who-" Edmund stopped himself. Didn't do to make demands of the CO.

"Yes. Haynes down at Hal Far, he's a chum. Was rather complimentary about your contribution to his fighter-bomber ops, even though he said you could be a bit stuffy at times."

"Hay-... Lieutenant-Commander Haynes? That's who mentioned me to you?"

"Yes. I wouldn't normally do this, you understand, but

given your reputation, I had concerns you were a glory hunter. I had a word with Joyce, your old CO too. He thought you were alright."

Nobody at the Admiralty, then? Edmund exhaled.

Haddow sat forward. "Why, who'd you think I meant?"

Edmund grinned sheepishly. "Well, the Assistant to the Second Sea Lord for starters. You don't have to go too far to find someone who'd happily see me given the chop. That whole business with the Morane on Madagascar put people's backs up. I'd have been annoyed too, if it happened to me."

"A couple of chaps did have a bee in their bonnet about that, to tell you the truth – goodness knows Clyde, you don't waste a lot of time making friends, do you? – but I ignored them. This is wartime, if it was my squadron I'd expect my pilots to swallow it and get on with their jobs."

"I suppose-"

"Suppose nothing. None of that matters. None of *us* matter. Only what we do up there. And as for that airliner... You did the right thing."

Edmund blinked. "I did?"

"Yes. Well, if you had shot it down, that would have been alright too, the Admiral had given his authorisation. But there were civvies on board and it's not your fault the pilot was an arsehole about it. The chances are the enemy knows we're here anyway. Nothing we can do about it. You made a decision in the heat of the moment – who knows if it was the best one? But you went about it the right way, you see? Kept your head, took a line and stuck to it. That's the main thing. And," the CO added with the closest thing to a smile Edmund had yet seen from him, "at least I know you aren't a glory hunter. That airliner was a sitting duck. You could've shot it down, but you didn't."

"Oh. Well as you put it like that..."

"We can't change it now, so we just have to focus on what we do next."

"I suppose, sir."

"And if anyone does kick up a stink, about that or about the other thing, then I'll back you up, of course."

Edmund stared. "Th-thank you sir."

"Oh for heaven's sake, call me Roger when we're not on squadron duty. Now sit down you silly bastard and let's make sure we're on top of everything. If they don't hit us today they're bound to tomorrow, and we won't have any margin for error."

The Storm

11 August 1942, morning

Edmund checked his watch. Oh-five-thirty. Almost time. His guts were churning, as they always did, even after all this time. Why couldn't the body learn, the way the mind could? Charlie was sitting on the upper cowling giving his windscreen a final polish, whistling an aria from The Marriage of Figaro like a virtuoso, trills and all. Edmund thought for a moment of striking up a conversation, something empty and distracting, but his tongue would not move. First light. The convoy had already moved out of night stations and looked oddly peaceful carving their white furrows in the slate waters. It was the peace of held breath.

Still, nobody had got lost. No sub or E-boat attacks. That was good. But it was a queer sort of game. The convoy had to win every round. The enemy just had to win one.

At least he'd got that business cleared up with Haddow. Good grief, what an idiot! His felt his face heat with the shame of it. How had he let it take control of him so? Of course, when he went to tell Vickery about it afterwards, the journalist had merely smiled and said "*Well, there you go then. A relief, I imagine?*" As if he'd known all along how things would turn out.

Start up!

Thank Christ. Edmund shook himself out of his reverie and finished the exterior checks, climbed into the cockpit, pumped a bit of ki-gas into the cylinders before hitting the button.

He'd allotted himself the first standing patrol. It felt like leading from the front. Was that it? Or was it that he couldn't bear the idea of sitting around waiting while the sun rose higher and every minute increased the stakes?

He felt the ship shift beneath him, a tilt only perceptible somewhere in the tides of his inner senses, as *Indomitable* turned into wind. A quick look over his shoulder to check Ambrose was ready, a smile that he hoped was reassuring, and then all there was to do was wait for the signal. There! Edmund opened the throttle, hand clamped on the brake lever, felt the Hurricane's tail rise, held for a moment as the forces balanced screaming engine, thrashing prop and stationary aircraft. Then release, and he was barrelling along the deck, feeling the wings' desperation to float the fighter skyward.

A glance in the mirror – yes, Ambrose was rolling – and a glance at the goofer's to see if Vickery was there – going too fast already, just a blur and in a moment the Hurricane was airborne. Wheels up, set throttle for best climb, checking again that Ambrose was on his quarter, and then up into the cloudless expanse.

Edmund forced himself to control his breathing. In, out... He could feel his heart thrumming with anticipation, and there was no sense in getting exhausted with nervous energy before the enemy even appeared.

The enemy. Were they out there?

Four fighters from *Indomitable* at high level and two from *Victorious* lower down...that was all that stood against them, to start off with. The radio hissed and the ADO was directing them to their station, 25,000 feet above the crawling ships.

Before they'd reached it, the radio crackled again. "Hello red leader, we have a plot. Single contact, looks like a snooper, eight miles out. Climb thirty thousand, steer zero-eight-five."

"Right, thirty thousand, zero-eight-five. On me, Ambrose. Keep your eyes peeled."

"Alright Clyde."

Just one snooper. OK, that was alright. Not hordes of Savoias and Junkers. Those would follow, though, if the snooper got his report in.

They passed through twenty thousand. It was getting cold. And harder to maintain the climb the higher they got. His new 'Z' was beginning to struggle, and he noticed Ambrose was somewhat higher now, twenty feet or so. Edmund resisted the urge to call him back. That extra bit might make a difference.

Higher, higher. Ambrose was sticking with him. Alright. Twenty-five thousand.

"Any news on that snooper?" Edmund barked. The controller was taking them the long way round, it seemed. Probably wanted to get them up-sun, but that meant steering east and cutting back. Edmund drummed his fingers on the spade grip. It was taking too long.

"Hold course and climb," the ADO replied after a pause.

"OK."

Blue Flight were in the air now too. Edmund listened to the ADO guiding them. Perhaps he was trying to catch the snooper in a pincer. He checked the altimeter. Just about thirty thousand. As soon as the needle touched the mark, he gently pushed the Hurricane level and felt the speed begin to pick up.

"Red Flight, steer three-four-zero, maintain current altitude."

Edmund acknowledged and nudged the Hurricane into a standard rate turn. Just as they were on the new course, the ADO's voice cut in again. "Steer two-eight-five, Red Flight, best speed. Bogey has turned west, now four miles west-sou'-west of you."

Damn, they were in a stern chase. They were already at full throttle. He could push it through the gate but he'd only get five minutes of overboost. Use it up too soon and he'd have none left for combat.

Edmund made a decision. "Line abreast Ambrose, a good distance, and keep your eyes peeled. Don't worry about our six o'clock, it's just us and the recce kite."

"Alright Clyde."

He divided up the sky and searched it, square by square. The light was about as good as it was going to get. They might see the bogey if it caught the sun. Sure enough, a flicker of orange briefly burned a little to the left.

"I see him. Turning to intercept." Edmund kept his eyes on the space where metal had flashed, and in a second they had picked out a mote moving across the blank western sky. "Still a couple of miles."

"Understood Red Leader," the ADO replied, "but keep to the north of him, it'll push him towards Blue Flight."

"Right-oh. Buster, Red Two." Edmund pushed the throttle through the gate, breaking the wire, and checked his watch. Five minutes. The Hurricane bucked and sprang forward. Ahead, the snooper evolved from a blob into a dash. God, it was moving alright. The shape began to resolve – a tick up behind was the tail, two thickenings were the engines slung beneath the wings. "Looks like a Junkers," he reported. Just then, the wings tilted and flashed again in the sun. Turning. "He just turned to the south, am pursuing."

Edmund heard the ADO giving more instructions to Blue Flight. He recognised Dickie Cork's voice in reply. He and Ambrose had barely gained on the Junkers when he spotted the stream of tracers, a puff of smoke, the tiny shape of a Hurricane forming a cross against the sky then plunging back into the attack. More smoke, a trail of it diving down to the east, Cork and Haworth chattering over the radio, *"There he goes!" "Did you see that, something flew off the port engine!" "Go on in you bastard!"* The scene receded to the east, and down, and Cork finally reported that they'd lost sight at about 200 feet.

Edmund throttled back, turned, and began orbiting over the convoy. Damn, it was cold. He hadn't been too aware of it until a moment or two ago, and now they'd have three quarters of an hour slowly chilling. But surely there would be more enemy aircraft soon – another snooper at the very least. Difficult to know if the Junkers had got off a report. Hell's Bells, this was intolerable!

The radio remained silent. There were no more contacts. Edmund and Ambrose hovered in the lightening sky as the convoy slowly crept out of shadow beneath. Wasn't even time for breakfast yet. The clock ran down, glacial. By the time the call came for them to return to *Indomitable*, all

Edmund could feel in his fingers was lances of pain. Then it was time to come in, and with a long, relieved exhalation that momentarily filled the cockpit with fog, Edmund began letting down towards the carrier.

He had the feeling back in his fingers and toes by the time *Indomitable* swam into view. Ambrose curved in to land, and settled down perfectly. Edmund's landing was tolerable. Only as he was climbing out of the cockpit did Edmund realise that the doped fabric patches over the gun ports were still intact. What was the bloody point of having four extra guns if he didn't bloody well use them?

He made a mental note to test the guns next time. It might not be all that important but it didn't do to come back with such an obvious sign of failure on the machine.

No, not failure. He clenched his jaw, forced down the disappointment. He and Ambrose had done exactly what was expected of them, and swept the Jerry into the waiting arms of Blue Flight. He'd better make sure Ambrose knew that, too.

And there would be other chances. There was time for tea, perhaps to force down a couple of mouthfuls of porridge, then he'd drop in to the FDO to listen in to whatever was happening. Haddow would be flying in a short while. Edmund's second stint would not be until the early afternoon.

He gave a monosyllabic interview to the IO, put in what could only at a stretch be called a 'combat report', and tried to find something that felt useful. There was nothing. The pilots all knew their job. The planning was all done. The mechanics would not benefit from being harangued.

The relief patrol flew off, and the standing patrol came back in. He spotted Vickery up on the island by an Oerlikon crew, and went up to exchange a few words about the earlier flight. There seemed little to say about it. There was the sky, vast, threatening, empty. "Why don't they come?" he snarled. "I wish they'd just bloody come."

Vickery smiled gently. "I understand. Why do you think they don't?"

Edmund snorted. "Why would they? They outnumber us four or five to one. They can just wait and come all at once. Then they can pummel us at their leisure. They'll have half a day at least within the range of their fighters, and that's more than enough to sink every merchantman here. Even with the numbers we've got, if they play it smart they can stop us without breaking a sweat."

"Hmm, I see." Vickery let the words hang, and for a moment there was nothing but the shush of the waves, the huffing of the wind around the radar aerials. Edmund had not put his fears into coherent form quite like that until now. It was sobering. "But still," Vickery added eventually. "During the Harpoon convoy. You stopped them then."

"Not me personally, I was in the drink."

The journalist laughed politely. "You know what I mean, though. And the Navy has learned from that?"

Edmund shook his head. "The enemy has too."

"Of course. But as hopeless as things may seem, there's a good chance of getting some of the ships through." Vickery folded his arms and regarded Edmund, challenging. "You made the point at the briefing yourself.

It doesn't take equal numbers to break up the enemy formations."

His own words. And he'd meant them. Edmund fought the temptation to roll his eyes. "I suppose you're right."

Vickery grinned triumphantly. "Not me. You. When are you back in the air?"

"Thirteen hundred."

"Alright, you have a little time then. Now, try and get some rest, I beg of you. There's no sense in getting worked up."

Edmund held up his hands. "OK, OK. What little rest there is for the wicked."

Just then, the tannoy boomed. *"Fighters, stand-to!"* A frenzy of activity burst on the flight deck like a bomb. Suddenly there were maintainers dashing in all directions, dragging trolley-accs, finishing checks. "Shadower approaching from the east-nor'-east. Pink section directed to intercept."

The activity on deck calmed somewhat. No sense in launching the stand-by fighters for a single aircraft. Edmund felt his hands tighten on the rail. After a while, the tannoy announced that the duty section was closing on the snooper, and then no more for another quarter of an hour. And then it was *"D'ye hear there? Pink section has driven the snooper away."*

Edmund cursed under his breath. He felt Vickery's gaze on him. Angling for an explanation. Good Lord, the man could use silence the way some could use a knife! He pursed his lips. "They're putting a gloss on it, but it means the fighters didn't catch the recce kite, so it's free to report our position and strength."

"I see." Vickery nodded slowly. He took a breath as if to expand, but what came out was simply "Oh! Look!"

Edmund followed his pointing finger. *Victorious*, on their port bow, half a mile away, was launching fighters, but there was a trail of smoke hanging in the air off the flight deck. Edmund traced it along. At the end of the trail was a Fulmar, curving round and turning downwind. Edmund's brows folded. Had his engine gone? At that moment, a lurid flicker illuminated the Fulmar's wing and more smoke bloomed.

"Ye Gods," Vickery muttered beside him. The Fulmar, sank towards the lethargic waves, still downwind, skimmed like a spun pebble off a crest and surged into the water.

"They're alright, they're alright," Edmund breathed, more as a prayer than an observation. The fighter hadn't broken up, hadn't sunk. "Didn't go in too badly considering. And the water'll put the fire out."

"Thank heaven. What do you think...?"

"Caused it? Can't say. My guess would be the ammunition went up. Every few rounds in a belt is an incendiary. Faulty round, could have set others off."

"Oh. Well, I suppose, thank goodness it happened so close to the water. I saw flamers in the last war. It's not..."

Edmund turned to look at Vickery. The journalist had gone very pale. Jesus. A fire in a wood-and-fabric aeroplane. It didn't bear thinking about. Of course, there was plenty of wood and fabric in a Hurricane, too... A destroyer was racing up between the carriers, flinging a wide arc of spray to either beam. They'd have the crew out in no time.

"Well, that's one more fighter down before we've even got into the fight," Edmund nodded towards the sinking Fulmar, whose tail was now well in the air. Yet oddly, he felt calmer than he had a few moments ago. The snooper would make its report – had probably already radioed it in. So the Germans and Italians would know exactly where they were. They would not have to waste time and fuel finding the convoy. Edmund realised his one hope that they might have got away relatively unscathed had gone, and with it, the anxiety. Now there was only the job. Only the fight. They would be equal to it, or they would not.

Edmund checked his watch. "They'll be flying the Spitfires for Malta off *Furious* any time now. Let's hope they all make it." He released his grip on the rail, nodded to Vickery, and took his leave. He could go and get his head down for half an hour. Read some Valéry, perhaps. Await the onslaught in peace.

11 August 1942, afternoon

No sooner had Edmund sat on his bunk and opened the book of verse than his eyelids began to droop. He rested the book on his chest and the next thing he registered was the thump as it slipped onto the floor. Good god, he was exhausted. He allowed his eyelids to sag again, but something stopped him from sleeping properly. There was too much noise, and something deep within his mind seemed determined to stay alert. Nevertheless, he made himself stay in repose until three quarters of an hour before it was time to fly. Then he splashed some water on his face and made his way to the hangar.

There was an atmosphere of controlled calm within the hangar, overlaying a palpable tension. They'd be busy in time, but as things stood, there was little to do.

"I had Bowers go over the ammo again," Charlie reported when Edmund found his aircraft. "Don't want a repeat of what happened with that Fulmar, eh?"

Edmund smiled wanly. "That was kind, thank you."

Charlie nodded. He didn't want his pilot going up like a Roman Candle any more than Edmund did. The deck crew were assembling so Edmund stood aside as they brought the aircraft to the lift, then rode with it to the flight deck. The breeze was less invigorating than usual. Edmund stretched his arms, rotated his shoulders. Would this be when the enemy showed up?

Calmly, efficiently, the crew readied the Red Section Hurris for launch. Edmund climbed aboard, the trolley-acc was hooked up, he flicked the magneto switches and pressed the starter. A fusillade of pops and bangs and the Merlin was singing in front of him, the needles on the gauges creeping to where they should be. The usual hot knot twisted in his guts. Every time. Would he never get used to it? Concentrate on the pre-flight, damn it, and soon you'll be too busy to be scared.

Something landed on his shoulder, tap tap, and the reflex kicked through him but it was only Charlie trying to attract his attention. Had he seen Edmund twitching? He pulled his flying helmet away from his ear.

"Not enough wind, sir, it'll have to be the accelerator,"

the rigger yelled.

"Alright." Edmund swallowed. Another thing he wasn't used to. *Eagle* didn't have an accelerator. He hadn't yet become accustomed to it. Perching right on the tip of the bow with nothing between him and the waves below if anything went wrong. At Charlie's signal he let off the wheel brakes and applied a blip of throttle, and another, just enough to unstick the Hurricane and get it rolling. He felt the deck party at the wingtips cajoling the Hurricane onto the right path, until he bumped up against the chocks. More hands were feverishly assembling the accelerator trolley.

At the forward end of the flight deck, the pitching of the carrier was nauseating. Oh Lord, the last thing he wanted was to throw up before he'd even got airborne. Best ignored. Ignore everything. Edmund started going through his cockpit checks again, while clunks and thuds reverberated through the airframe as the deck crew hooked up the carriage. There was a vertiginous rising sensation – nothing wrong, it was just the tail being hoisted into the air so the rear arms could be attached. Now he could see right over the nose, straight into the malachite waves. Edmund swallowed again, tasting something bitter and chemical. *Indomitable* seemed to be twisting as well as pitching. A ghastly corkscrew. Edmund looked down at the Hurricane's footboards.

Just then, the spade grip flapped to the left, then the right, then left again. Edmund let out a bark. Some damned fool was waggling the ailerons. He looked out and Charlie was standing by the wingtip, waving, jabbing his hand at something behind him over to port.

Oh, heavens! *Eagle*, which had been steaming alongside *Indomitable*, was shrouded in smoke and fumes. For a second, Edmund could not make sense of the scene. There were the ships of the fleet, sparking in the sun, throwing jewels of spray into the air, and a pall of smoke that did not fit with anything, as though a volcano had suddenly appeared in the middle of the Mediterranean. And then another gout of black smoke issued from the carrier, jets of white steam, a patter of concussions thumping deep within his skull.

Eagle had been hit. The thought struck him in the midriff before it reached his head. *Eagle*. Hit. But there wasn't a bomber in the sky!

A submarine. Christ.

The smoke began to thin, and for a glorious moment everything was going to be alright, and then, and then... A strip of red of Eagle's hull antifouling was visible, then more of it. The carrier's island was leaning away. She was turning turtle.

All his old shipmates. Mac, Joe and Tony, his old rigger and fitter and armourer. Tricky, the controller. Spike and Crosley. The other swine from the squadron who'd tormented him. The fish-head officers who'd looked down their noses. They were all over there, on that leaning ship. *Eagle* was slewing round now, the bows turning towards him. Edmund felt a tightness in his shoulders and realised he was trying to push against his harness to see better. The port edge of the flight deck was already skimming the water. As he watched, a Hurricane slithered down the slope and plopped into the sea, disappearing without a ripple. Bile flooded his mouth. Hope to Christ the pilot had got out before... Oh Lord, the whole ship was going over. But no, the roll seemed to stop as the flight deck dipped into the waves, and it was the bow that was going down.

Somebody do something! But they were, a destroyer was racing towards the carrier. There was a clatter of movement and Charlie was standing on the wing root, hanging on the cockpit canopy rail. "Need to get going sir, there are U-boats around – let Wings know the second you're ready!"

Edmund couldn't make his voice work, but nodded vigorously. Oh God, at any moment *Indomitable* might suffer the same fate as *Eagle*. The Hurricane sliding down the deck and into the fathomless deep would be his. The pilot would be him. His palms were cold, oily with sweat. He wiped them on his shorts, leaving ugly smears. Checks complete, he gave the thumbs up. Barely was his hand back on the spade grip before the DCO dropped his flag and with a great shove in the back, a lurching nod forward, the Hurricane was at flying speed and nothing below the wheels but sea.

After that, the flight was an anti-climax. Not even a snooper probing the outer flanks of the convoy. They hardly needed to! The convoy was wearing out its own defences and ships were being picked off. They were being softened up for the death blow.

One of the other aircraft reported a torpedo track crossing in front of *Victorious*. Edmund held his breath as they called it in. The convoy changed course, the destroyers raced about hurling depth charges into the impassive waters.

Why don't they come!

You know why.

At the end of the patrol, Edmund and Ambrose let down from the icy 25,000 feet to a balmy five thousand, and entered the pattern.

"What's that at two o'clock, level, Clyde?" Ambrose's voice scratched through the radio. "A fighter I think, can't see if it's one of ours."

Edmund eased the throttle forward. In a moment he could see it was a Hurricane. In another moment he caught a glimpse of the fuselage code. It was one of *Eagle*'s!

"Hello Pedestal, there's a Hurri on his own, tell him to come in and we'll wait."

"Belay that," came a voice through his headphones before the ADO could respond. "I'm not coming in until the standing patrol is down. I'm losing oil and can't see properly."

"You're cleared to land on *Indomitable*, Black Two." The ADO's voice was sharp. "Come in immediately."

"Not bloody likely. What if I crash on deck? You two come past me. Don't argue now, we're just wasting time."

The ADO acquiesced, and in another couple of minutes, Clyde and Ambrose were back aboard *Indomitable*. They stood watching as the Hurricane came closer, crabbing awkwardly so the pilot could see ahead, and eventually curving tightly onto final approach. The wheels thumped down, the hook caught and though it was rough, it was still a better landing than Clyde had managed after the training exercise those endless weeks ago. The pilot climbed from the cockpit, scooped his flying helmet from his head and stopped, face to face with Edmund.

"Bloody hell, it's you! Clydesdale!"

Edmund forced a smile. "Hello Geoffreys. Good to see you. So you were in the air when *Eagle*...when she was hit, then?"

The pilot's eyes widened even further. "Have you heard anything? How many got out?"

"I don't know. A lot, I think." he tried to sound nonchalant. It didn't seem to come out that way. "She didn't go down that fast. And there were destroyers in attendance almost immediately."

"Oh. Right. You saw it?"

"Yes. I was on the accelerator. Waiting to launch."

"Oh. Grandstand seat, then. God, I hope the escorts got the bastards who sunk her! Did they, do you think?" His head swivelled around for a moment, eyes wide, before his gaze settled back on Edmund. "Well, you still have the luck of the devil then, I see. What are you doing here?"

"Eight-hundred needed a Senior Pilot."

"Is that right?" He issued a slight snort. "I heard you'd been court martialled."

Edmund laughed, a metallic sound that surprised him. "Not yet. With any luck the Jerries will get me first, eh Geoff?"

Geoffreys nodded. He hadn't seemed to have heard. "So, you're Splot, you say?" he said after a moment. "Get me another kite, would you? I need to fly again."

The day wore on. Every minute brought them closer to

Malta, and closer to the relative safety of darkness. Every minute brought them closer to the hundreds of torpedo planes, bombers and Stukas that awaited them. There were no more alarms. The sinking of *Eagle* had not presaged a mass U-boat attack. Just one lucky sub, then, luckily placed and probably with a lucky shot. It couldn't happen again, could it? He went for a word with Haddow and raised Geoffreys' request.

"What do you reckon?" Haddow asked. "There's nothing much happening at the moment, and Barnes could do with a rest. He looks as though he's going to throw up. We'll need him on the top line for tomorrow."

Edmund rubbed the back of his neck. It made him uneasy to muck about with carefully constructed plans, but Haddow had a point about Barnes, and Geoff would no doubt kick up a stink if he was denied. "Alright, I'll put him as number two to Brierly and move Gordon to Yellow, how's that?"

"Fine. Get it done."

Edmund found the pilots and filled them in, introduced Geoff to Brierly and went to see that the stand-by flight, waiting since the last duty flight had taken off, were all set. He sent a rating to make sure they at least had something to drink and a biscuit or two to munch on while they sat waiting, and after a while a couple of off-watch stokers brought out a fannie of lukewarm tea and started slopping it into tin mugs, handing out biscuits. The pilots sat in their cockpits, occasionally stretching or standing to look around, peering at the anxious sky. Mechanics sat on trolley-accs or lounged on deck. Haddow came out and stood, hands thrust in his pockets, to check all was well.

Like cold water to the face, Edmund realised the CO was nervous. Haddow nodded aft. "Look at that bird on the staff. Ugly blighter."

Edmund turned his head. A huge gull was sitting atop the crown. It levelled a bilious eye at them.

"An Italian spy, probably," Haddow added.

"He looks unimpressed by us, I'd say."

"Can you blame him?"

Edmund laughed. "Yes, actually. He can go and bother *Victorious*, that'll give him a sense of perspective. Go on, you swine. *Hoosh*!"

The gull looked at them appraisingly again, and shifted from one foot to the other.

"We ought to use it for target practice. I wish I'd brought my revolver up here."

Edmund suppressed a snort. "Probably best not. Might be bad luck."

"Isn't that only for an albatross?"

"It'd be bad luck for anyone you hit by mistake."

Haddow gaped theatrically. "Oi! I was going to recommend you for a gong, but I shan't bother now. You're hardly one to talk. You can barely hit the flight deck with a Hurricane."

"I'm never going to be allowed to forget that landing, am I?" Edmund tutted and shook his head.

"Not as long as I draw breath."

They sagged into silence at that, looking into space, not knowing what else to do. "Honestly, if they keep us waiting much longer, I'm going to write a very stiff letter to Mussolini," Edmund said, trying to sound jaunty. "It's terrible service."

Haddow looked at him sidelong. "Don't you know there's a war on?"

Edmund made sure to catch the pilots of each flight as they left the debrief, offering a word of encouragement, asking if there was anything they needed. Most just seemed frustrated. Knowing there would be a fight to come, just wanting to get on with it. Edmund couldn't blame them.

The afternoon watch changed to the first dog watch, and then the second. Eighteen hundred hours. The light started to fade. Might they get away with it?

Then, the sound of muffled reports reached them on the breeze. Everyone listened. Then someone pointed. Right over on the forward port edge of the destroyer screen, puffs of black smoke high in the deepening blue.

Well, well. Caught on the bloody hop! *Indomitable* was sheering into wind, the stand-by flight Hurricanes seeming to strain at the leash. Brierly and Geoff. So much for putting Geoff in for a quiet spell. Oh, why hadn't they come when Edmund was in the air?

The black puffs crept closer, working diagonally towards the ships. He peered up at them. Some of the tiny black spots up there must be aircraft, but it was impossible to tell them apart from the anti-aircraft fire. Then, he saw the guns start working on HMS *Phoebe* nearby, belching smoke and pumping back and forth in incongruous silence until the noise reached him over the carrier's engines and bow wave.

"Look!", someone shouted, "they're going for *Victorious*!"

Edmund turned to where the other carrier surged along, away on their port bow, and above, three knots of tiny black crosses, now unmistakeable as aircraft, had detached from the main mass he had just been looking at. They'd curved apart and were converging on the carrier from different directions. *Victorious* heeled, her wake churning white as she turned into the attack, then lurched back into a zig-zag. The AA guns tore out in renewed fury, but the bombers kept on, now losing height. He held his breath. They were surely overhead *Victorious* now. The carrier reversed her turn yet again, the hull leaning hard, and the first bombs were blasting at empty water, hurling foam into towers. A cluster of columns burst between *Victorious* and *Indomitable* and for a moment the other carrier had disappeared, swallowed by the furious detonations. Everyone stared, fixing on the forest of waterspouts as they reached a peak and began to melt, and, heaven be praised, the hull emerged intact from the maelstrom and a cheer boomed out from *Indomitable*'s deck.

The air was filled with solid noise. The bombers – Edmund could see they were Junkers 88s now – carved away, their job done, but the Hurricanes were on them, and another whoop erupted from *Indomitable*. Those are our lads! The fighters were weaving and bobbing, fastening on the last in a group, falcons harrying a gamebird. There was a bright flash in the heart of the bomber and in the next moment it was cartwheeling downward, half its wing missing, making orange circles of flame in the dusk until it lanced noiselessly into the sea. Three, no, four, mushrooms blossomed in the sky, silhouetted against the orange glow to the west, and began drifting downward, swaying gently in the faltering breeze. Parachutes.

Further ahead, though, more bombs fell, white columns sprouting in clusters, new ones appearing just as the old ones began to dissipate. The thump of detonations began to reach the carrier's deck over the clatter of AA fire. Above, the densest patch of AA puffs revealed that the main body of bombers was still intact. On the far side of the convoy, guns began to blaze. A low-level attack was developing. Edmund heaved a breath in, swallowed against the nausea rising. Powerless to do anything!

The light really was fading. The destroyers of the screen were all but hidden in gloom. The patches of waterspouts began to thin. In another three or four minutes, there was no more than the occasional stray burst. The mass of bombers above was thinning too, moving away in small groups, harried by knots of pom-pom and 4.5 inch bursts.

Edmund exhaled. That looked to be the last of it. Had all the merchantmen survived? Well, there was nothing he could do about that now. And with the light going, they had to get the fighters back on deck right now. He made a move to run to the FDO, but stopped himself. They knew their jobs and would be bringing the boys back. Sure enough, in a few minutes, the tannoy crackled and Wings was calling for the flight deck to be cleared. Edmund headed for the goofers' gallery, and was not in the least bit surprised to find Vickery up there along with a jostling crowd of off-watch gawkers.

"Here they come." Edmund pointed for Vickery's benefit, at the first fighter appeared in the landing circuit. One by one they came in, Edmund counting them off. The sun was already down.

"Christ, I wouldn't like to land in this murk," the journalist murmured. Edmund could only agree. The pilots who'd been up were clearly beginning to struggle. He noticed one Hurricane from *Victorious* touched down, and saw the pilot's bewilderment at climbing out of the cockpit and realising he was on the wrong ship. That would have made all their aircraft back, but now he realised there was one missing. He hadn't seen 6-L yet. That was Barnes' machine, but... He cursed softly.

"What's the matter?" Vickery asked. "Aren't they all back? I thought..."

"The last one isn't one of ours. Oh, Lord. Well, he might have put down on *Victorious*, I suppose." The deck ahead of the barrier was looking pretty full by now. There was one more aircraft curving round, into the approach. Edmund's heart lifted for a second, then plunged as he recognised it was a Fulmar. The two-seater steadied. Edmund glimpsed the batsman, gripping a pair of torches instead of the usual bats, waving frantically. The Fulmar was a little too high but 'Bats' brought it down. Until the last second, everything was fine. Edmund breathed out, and then the ship nodded in a slightly larger than usual pitch, the Fulmar seemed to settle on the air and float a little... It touched down between the third and fourth wires, the wheels bounced, and in sickening slow motion, the fighter ballooned up, drifted forward, the last unattainable couple of feet passed between the arrestor hook and the wires, carrying it right into the barrier.

The first wire sliced the wheels off and threw the nose up, and the Fulmar, still skimming like a paper plane, skidded onto the second barrier. The steel cable shredded the propeller, shrieked as the aircraft scraped across it, still half-flying, and cannoned into the parked Hurricanes waiting to be taken below.

Edmund threw his arm across his face, as the graunching of metal on metal reached a crescendo, but the Fulmar didn't explode or burst into flame. The fire crews were already dousing it with foam. It finally stopped, halfway up the mangled tail of a Hurricane, which had in turn crumpled the wing of another.

"Bollocks," Edmund snapped. Three fighters down in one fell swoop. *Eagle* gone, and now this. He saw Brierly sprinting for the island and shouted to him.

"Did you see that?" The pilot yelled. "Bloody truck driver from *Vic* buggered my kite!"

"We'll find you another, don't you worry," Edmund called back, though he had no idea whether that was true or not. "Did you see what happened to Geoff from *Eagle*? He's not back."

Brierly shrugged. "Sorry, old man. Last I saw of him he was pursuing a crowd of Ju 88s back to Sardinia. I called and called for him to break off..."

Edmund swallowed and nodded. "Go and get a mug of cocoa, I'll see you in the debrief. And thanks."

He turned and caught Vickery looking at him, impassive. "I should never have let him go back up," Edmund choked.

"It's my fault."

12 August 1942, morning

An hour before sunrise and the hangar was still cacophonous with activity. It had been that way since the previous evening. Two aircraft seriously damaged when the Fulmar crashed into them, three damaged in combat. The Fulmar itself was a wreck, and once it had been extricated from the Hurricanes, was tipped over the side. At least the crew were unharmed, and a Walrus was coming to pick them up at first light.

"How's it going Charlie?" Edmund shouted to his rigger, who sighed and put down his spanner.

"Getting there, sir. Just tidying up, now. We'll have a full set of machines for you to take up." He pointed at one Hurricane where maintainers were swarming around the aft end, another where they were doing likewise at the nose. "That one's had had a complete new tail assembly fitted, the one behind it's had a new wing. That one over there's having a new propeller, and the crew's been up all night fixing a right bugger of a hydraulic leak."

"You're miracle-workers, all of you," Edmund said. He felt a twist of guilt at seeing Geoff's old aircraft among the repaired machines. Odd that it had survived and its pilot hadn't. "You all deserve a medal as far as I'm concerned."

"Thank you sir, that's nice to hear," Charlie replied, evidently trying hard to overcome his embarrassment. "How are we doing in general?"

Edmund grimaced, and immediately wished he hadn't. "Not too bad all told. The main blow was *Eagle* going down. Four of her Hurris were in the air, the rest went with her." The sight of it. Good God. He still didn't know how many people they'd lost. How many pilots and maintainers and officers he knew were no longer on this plane of existence... He noticed Charlie staring and realised he'd trailed off. "Er, we lost a couple of Fulmars and a Hurri from Vic too. As far as I can make out, we're about twenty fighters down on this time yesterday. About fifty left."

"That'll do, won't it?" Charlie's usual confidence had deserted him.

"It'll have to." Edmund checked his watch. "Right. I'd better be off. Flying with the first patrol again."

"Good luck sir." The rigger's smile was back. "Bag us a nice lot of Huns won't you, I want to paint some crosses on your new kite."

Edmund smiled, thanked Charlie again and departed. Once he'd seen the early patrol flown off – two aircraft at sun-up, just in case – he headed for the ready room. Brierly was already there when he arrived. "Everything alright Ken?" he asked. "You're not up until the forenoon watch are you?"

"Ah, Clyde, I wanted to have a word, if you don't mind." He shuffled his feet and looked aside for a second. "Look, I'm terribly sorry about Geoffreys. I honestly did everything I could. He just latched on to those bombers and wouldn't break off."

Edmund grimaced, dragged his hand through his hair. "Not your fault, Ken. I shouldn't have let him take Barnes' kite. I s'pose he was hit harder by *Eagle* sinking than I realised."

"Ah yes, quite possible. I didn't know either, he just seemed keen."

They both stood, nodding, avoiding each other's gaze for a moment.

"Ah, that wasn't what I wanted to say, though," Brierly added after a moment. "Well, not the main thing."

"Oh?" Edmund looked up. Trouble? He waved Brierly to go on.

Brierly pursed his lips and frowned. He seemed to be working something out in his head. "It's the direction," he said eventually. "I'm not sure it's working."

"How do you mean?

"Yesterday evening, *Vic*'s ADO took an age getting us into position, and when he did, it was the wrong position." Brierly hunched forward and lowered his voice. "He had us all get up-sun, but by the time he did, the sun had about gone."

"So it was pointless?"

"Worse than that. We were silhouetted beautifully against the dusk, while we had real trouble seeing the bombers. We mostly only got to them after they'd dropped their bombs."

"Hmm. I see what you mean. It did look a bit haphazard from down here." Edmund thought for a moment. There wasn't much time to address it. None, really, he was supposed to be flying soon. And perhaps it was just because of the lack of daylight. "Have you spoken to Commander Haddow?"

"No, didn't want to bother the Old Man with it." He smiled sheepishly. "And of course, chain of command and so on."

Edmund mustered a wan smile in return. "Of course. It's a pretty complicated business you know, I'm sure they're doing their best. Look, I'm flying in a minute but I'll keep an eye on things and see if there's still a problem, alright?"

"Yes, I suppose."

Edmund pulled himself up. It didn't do to dismiss a pilot's concerns, not when they'd taken the step of consulting a senior officer. "But here's what," he added. "I really should tell you to go and get some rest, but I don't suppose you'll be able to while this is preying on your mind, so why don't you see if you can speak to a couple of the other lads who were flying yesterday evening and check if they concur? Then we'll compare notes when I get back down."

Brierly brightened. "Alright Clyde, will do. Good hunting."

As Edmund's Hurricane roared into the air and climbed away from the carrier, he felt his spirits lifting. There'd be a dozen fighters up there now. Enough to buy the convoy a bit of time when the raids came.

"Make angels two-five and steer three-one-zero Red Leader," the ADO ordered. "Plots on the board already."

"Understood. Angels two-five, heading three-one-zero. On me, red and green flights."

As the pilots told off one by one, Edmund tuned to the north east, set the throttle for best climb and scanned the sky ahead. This was it!

"Small group of high-level bombers approaching convoy from the north-west," the ADO informed him. The two pairs of Sea Hurricanes split up, aiming to catch the bombers if they dodged. There was a hell of a lot of sky up here, and a lot of gaps that small groups of aircraft could dodge through. Was this how it was going to be?

In a second, the radio spluttered again. "Bring heading to zero-five-zero, Red Leader."

Edmund acknowledged and turned onto the new course. Still no sign of those bombers.

"Hullo Red Leader, hullo red leader. Do you see them yet? You should see 'em any minute, now three to four miles north of the convoy port wing. Twenty-two thousand."

"Nothing yet, Pedestal. Bearing, please?"

There was a pause, then another hiss, and faintly, "Three tri-motors, two o'clock low, Tally Ho Black Flight!"

"Sorry, Red Leader. Bearing One-seven-two."

There was a flurry of chatter from the low cover making its interception. Edmund hauled the Hurricane onto its new course. Finally! A gaggle of twin-engined bombers about a mile ahead, cutting diagonally from left to right.

"There they are, eleven o'clock low. Four Junkers. With me Red Two, quarter attack, Tally Ho!"

Edmund shoved the throttle through the gate, uncaring about the rough handling his engine was taking, and pointed the nose down a touch. The Hurricane kicked and picked up speed. He flicked on the reflector sight, adjusted it to the right span for a Ju 88, and checked the guns' safety was off. At six hundred yards nothing was happening. The range closed. Six-fifty. Five hundred. He thumbed the button, saw the tracers going a little aft, adjusted, pushed it again, and played the guns on the middle of the last bomber. Damn it, don't get too close...had to remember his own advice! Edmund heaved the Hurricane into a bank and then a curving turn away from the bombers, down and to starboard, out of the reach of the guns that were only now starting to fire in return.

"Everything OK Ambrose?" he panted through the G-force in the turn.

"OK Red Leader," the other pilot croaked, the strain in his voice audible.

Edmund pushed the rudder, reversing the turn, setting the two Hurricanes on a course back toward the pack of Junkers, and as the ring of the reflector sight drifted onto the last aircraft, opened fire again. The twelve guns rattled in unison, Edmund feeling them judder through the airframe, seeing the tracers pour out towards the Junkers. Crikey, it helped having four more guns! He caught a glimpse of bright splashes around the nearer engine, and was that something falling off? And then it was time to sheer away before the defensive fire got too fierce.

This time, he ducked to port and curved down under the bombers – don't make it too predictable, he thought – and came back in from slightly underneath. The tracers from the bombers were streaming by, not too close at first, but creeping nearer. And then he was firing back, a little wide, but then the rounds were striking, flashing and puffing on the bomber's belly.

The four Junkers had started to spread out, to weave gently, but it wasn't enough to throw the Hurricanes off their aim. Just as Edmund led Red section in for a third time, he saw the bomb bay doors open, and clusters of dark shapes tumbling down. Blast! He gave the aftermost bomber the last of his ammunition, and turned away, with a glance back to check they hadn't downed any with their final effort. He caught a glimpse of a thin streak of smoke, but the aircraft were still together.

"Any ammo left, Red Two?" Edmund asked when they'd put a bit of distance between themselves and the bombers.

"Nothing I'm afraid," Ambrose replied. "To be honest, I'd run out before that last pass."

"OK. Try to keep your bursts short next time. Good work. Did you hit anything?"

"A bit. You damaged one. I saw him start smoking, and I think one of his undercart doors fell off."

Edmund felt a moment's satisfaction, immediately overwhelmed. They hadn't brought any aircraft down, and they hadn't stopped them from bombing. Christ. A glimpse of a vision of bombs, wobbling in the airstream, plunging away, and he offered up a prayer none of them had hit anything, that at the very least he and Ambrose had thrown the bombers off their aim.

Edmund throttled back and pointed the nose down, telling the ADO they were out of ammo and were returning. They might not be able to land just yet, but there was no use hanging about up here wasting petrol.

By the time they reached *Indomitable*, the carrier was curving into wind to launch the next relief patrol. They went straight in. Edmund's machine was undamaged. Ambrose's had a couple of bullet holes in one wingtip, easily patched. They went to the IO and made their reports. Ambrose confirmed his claim for a Junkers 88 damaged, for all that was worth. The overall picture was dismaying. Only two interceptions had been made, only one of which resulted in a confirmed kill – the Fulmars, with their low-level CANT torpedo bomber. With an overwhelming wash of relief, Edmund heard that no ships had been hit.

Still, Edmund felt a sick sensation spreading deep in his midriff. Brierly was right. The tactics were all wrong. They had the means of at least a chance of victory, and they were throwing it away.

He stomped to the ready room. Brierly was there, looking as though he were dancing on hot bricks.

"Well?" The pilot demanded. "How did it go?"

"Not terrible. But it could've been a lot better. Did you find anyone who'd back you up?"

"Oh yes! Simner, Warr and Higginbotham. I can go and get 'em if you like."

Edmund waved the offer away. "Never mind that, you'll just have to speak for them. Come on, we need to put this to Haddow."

They found the CO in the Air Direction Office, seemingly deep in conversation with Walpole, and asked for a word. Haddow slipped into the passageway, closing the door behind him, and eyed the two pilots suspiciously. "Well?"

"We wanted a word about the tactics, sir," Edmund started.

Haddow folded his arms. "What about them?"

Edmund took a breath. "It's not good enough. We aren't

breaking up the raids."

"He's right sir," Brierly broke in. "We aren't getting close 'til it's too late."

"Come on Clyde. Ken. It's a bit late to start mucking about with the plan now. All we can do is give it our best shot. We can't work miracles with what we've got."

"You don't-" Edmund took a breath. The words had come out shriller than he'd intended. He pushed back the pressure building in his chest, but it was all coming out in a rush. "You don't understand. You haven't seen it. Last time out only two ships got in. It was enough to tide them over for a few weeks, but that was all. They're starving to death and being bombed to fragments. They need the food and they need the petrol for the fighters. There won't be a next time. All these ships have to get through. All of them! And we have to give the bombers enough of a bloody nose that they can't just toddle over to Grand Harbour and sink them before they've unloaded."

Haddow folded his arms, raised an eyebrow. "My responsibility is to my squadron, you know that Clyde. After this battle there'll be another, and another."

"Not for Malta there won't," Edmund replied, hating the petulance in his voice. "I mean it. Another result like Harpoon and they're as good as finished. These beam and quarter attacks aren't doing the trick. We have to do it differently."

"Well what do you suggest?"

"Head-on, right into the formations. Break 'em up and then pick off the bombers one by one."

"And the fighters?"

Edmund shrugged. "Ignore them. Dodge as best we can. If we get tangled up with the fighters, the bombers *will* get through."

Haddow looked at him with narrowed eyes for far longer than Edmund liked. "Alright," he said eventually. "We'll do it your way. I'll have a word with Wings and get *Vic*'s ADO to position us head-on. But it'll be your job to sell it to the pilots. They need to know that if they fluff it on the way in, it'll probably be the last mistake they make."

"I know, I know. On my head be it."

"It's not though, is it Clyde?" Haddow said softly. "It's all of us."

The 800 Squadron pilots assembled in the ready room – those who weren't already in the air – with a smattering from 880, too. There was an air of uneasiness. Or was that suspicion? It was still only a quarter to nine, and Edmund felt as though he'd been up for days.

"Alright chaps," he started. "No time for beating about the bush, so I'll get right to it. We don't think the tactics we were using last night and this morning are working."

There was a murmur from the pilots, no more than that. Agreement? Or annoyance.

"Trying to work up sun of the enemy and attack from the rear is taking too long, and it's not affecting the integrity of their formations. Yesterday we only caught one of their bombers, and that was after it had attacked the convoy. It was the same this morning. Now, as I said before, the number of kills don't matter, but we need to break 'em up. It's imperative that the formations be made to shatter, so each bomber is forced to go it alone, and we don't get a concentrated mass of aircraft over the target where they're bound to hit something."

He paused to let that sink in. He seemed to have their attention, anyway.

"So here's what we propose to do. Instead of working around behind the enemy aircraft, we climb to height as quickly as possible, and go at 'em head on. Straight down the barrel."

There was a ripple then, which rose to a hubbub. He waited for quiet.

"The ADOs have been given their instructions. They'll do their best to get you there with a height advantage. And the good news is that the sun's high enough and south enough that you won't be attacking right into it. But neither will you have its protection. On the other hand, the Ju 88s and Savoias we'll be facing don't have much forward-facing armament. They won't like getting a flight of Sea Hurricanes in the face. Some of them will break before you get there. Once the first head-on attack has been made, if the formation hasn't broken up, we can still circle back and make quartering attacks. But I'll bet my life they will break up. It worked in 1940, and their bomber pilots haven't got any braver since then."

Not that Edmund had much experience of such an attack in anger. But the others didn't have to know that...

"You've covered it in training, so you know the basics. You'll need to open fire a bit earlier because of the closing speed. The main thing to remember is to hold your course, and your nerve. Pick an aircraft and don't break, don't even jink, until the last second. Give them a squirt, but let them break first. I'd recommend passing above or below rather than to one side or the other – which depends on if you're coming in from above or below. Use your instinct, it'll serve you."

"What about collisions?" someone snapped. He couldn't see who, not that it mattered.

"Not very likely," he retorted. "It's bloody difficult to hit another machine head on with a closing speed of five hundred, even if you're trying to. If there's any lead at all, it's damn near impossible. There's a bit of a risk, of course, but it balances out – less return fire in the initial run-in, and if they break up, if we do our jobs right, their defences lack all co-ordination." He softened his tone a little. "I know this is a tough proposition, but we only get one chance. It's today. Now or never. Malta's fate is in our hands. Let's go and take it."

There was apprehension there in their faces. Fear, even. But also a glint of determination.

"Everyone clear? Alright, duty section on deck in ten, the rest of you, see you in the air."

There was a rumble of affirmation, and the pilots began to stand, head for the door in ones and twos, muttering, a few staying put and leaning back in their chairs, grabbing a magazine or paperback. Haddow nodded to him from the back, just once, and left, but immediately Edmund's shoulders felt freed of a mass that had been bearing down on them. Edmund was about to leave when he noticed a figure in a chair in the far corner.

"Honestly," Edmund said. "Are there any confidential

briefings you won't sneak in to?"

Vickery chuckled. "I've got this far without being arrested. It would be a shame to lose my record so close to retirement." He leaned forward. "That was a good speech, by the way. Short and sweet."

"D'you reckon it worked?"

The journalist shrugged. "We'll know in about twelve hours' time."

***

The new standing patrol flew off, and the last one recovered. Edmund filled the pilots in on the new tactics.

No more than a couple of minutes later, the tannoy boomed, "*D'ye hear there? Formation of enemy bombers inbound from the north-east. Standby flight ready.*"

Here we go, then. Edmund hit the starter and his Hurricane clattered into life, darts of flame shooting from the exhaust stubs. As he took off he could hear the ADO positioning the duty flight in the path of the bombers. Good heavens, he'd better be right! It looked promising, anyway. The first wave of fighters hit the bombers when they were still 25 miles out from the convoy. Edmund listened to the shouts and whoops over the radio, willing his Hurricane to climb a little faster.

He didn't even need the ADO to find the battle. It was there, dead ahead, expanding and distorting like a murmuration of starlings. As he drew closer, he made out two loose packs of bombers, frayed and irregular, losing cohesion even as he watched. Fighters wheeled around the edges, tracers scoring the sky.

Edmund picked the closer, right-hand group. "Red and

White flights, this is Red Leader. Loosen formation."

The Hurricanes began to spread out, creating room to manoeuvre.

"Head on, now. Stay with me. Find a target, give them a spray and miss by as little as you dare. Tally Ho!"

He shoved the throttle wide, hung on, and picked a Junkers right in the middle. It was coming on fast, just a little lead, drifting to the left. Edmund thumbed the gun button for an instant, just to see where the tracers were going, corrected a touch... the bomber was rushing up, only a couple of seconds to get it right, and he mashed the button and held it down while the guns erupted either side of him, sending streams of ammo hurtling towards the target. The bomber was coming on, ludicrously fast, and he shoved the stick forward, feeling the Hurricane buck, somewhere in his brain he registered the Junkers just starting to bank. A check in the mirror, a glance to either side, just to make sure the others were with him, and he pulled into a wide left turn.

"Red and White Flights, everyone OK?" he panted as the G started loading up, shoving at his shoulders.

Each of them replied, all had made it through. "That was bracing," Brierly added, not quite sotto voce. As the turn continued, bringing them back around towards the bombers, Edmund noticed with triumph that the formation was bursting apart like a flock of birds after a sudden shot. It worked!

"Red Leader. Pick a target and help yourself."

In a moment the airwaves were full of shouts. Edmund picked a Junkers that was trying to weave and falling behind the main pack, barrelling in at its side, plying the cockpit with tracers. The bomber lurched, and began to sink, the nose falling a little, then a little more. "You don't get out of it that easily," he snarled, jinking aside, then turning back, giving the Junkers another long burst. The dive steepened, and he was in danger of overtaking, so he pulled the prop into fine pitch. The Junkers was in an almost vertical dive now. Edmund felt the controls loading up under his hands and feet. He was about to fire again when the bomber's port mainplane began to tremble and, as if it were no more than the wing of a daddy-long-legs, peeled away, followed a second later by the starboard wing, which fluttered like feathers, while the fuselage speared downward into oblivion.

Edmund throttled back and gently pulled the Hurricane out of the dive, then eased the throttle open again and used the momentum of the dive to slingshot the aircraft back up again. He'd lost a good few thousand feet and had got separated from the fight. He scanned the sky rapidly, and found the area scarred by smoke and vapour trails.

He realised his ears were full of chatter and his clothes soaked in sweat. It was suddenly cold. "Keep the air clear," he barked into the radio. Nobody took any notice.

And then, *"they're turning back!"* And *"bastards are ditching their bombs!"*

Edmund laughed in relief as he watched the bombers, now completely disorganised, turning tail.

"This is Red Leader, let them go," he ordered. "Return to mother, refuel and rearm."

Once they'd recovered to the ship, they climbed out of

their Hurricanes and Edmund had a quick look at each to check for damage. All OK. Phew! Ambrose was standing by his machine, so still and so white he might have been carved from marble. Edmund called him, then again. The third time, his head turned. "Hmm?"

"I said, everything alright Ambrose? You're not hurt?"

The glass sheen on the pilots eyes blinked away. "Oh. No. No, no. Fine."

"What happened?"

Ambrose stared at him for a second, as a man might stare at a crossword clue in the hope that the answer will resolve itself. "I went after a Junkers. I kept hitting it and hitting it. Nothing was happening. The gunner was dead, I could see that. But the thing just kept on flying. So I gave him burst after burst. And then. It was the strangest thing."

Edmund released his breath gently. "Go on."

"There was a sort of glow. Up by the cockpit. Couldn't work it out. Sort of a yellow glow. Not like a flare exactly. It kept growing, spreading out over the fuselage."

Edmund swallowed. "Ah. And then?"

"I didn't know what it was until... Smoke. There was a puff of smoke. Well it was on fire, you see. Fire. The whole thing was ablaze from stem to stern. They were trying to get out, but..." He had been looking toward Edmund, as though there was no-one there, as if Edmund were invisible, or a mirror. Something in his eyes flickered and he was looking at Edmund again. "I thought it was the most beautiful thing I'd ever seen."

The young pilot turned away, doubled over, his head jerked, and a gush of vomit splashed on the deck, then another, and another, until Ambrose stood, contorted, grunting and heaving for breath, his body struggling to eject what it could not. "Sorry sir," he panted when he had reasserted control.

"That's alright. Go and drink some water. Maybe get some milk if you can find it. Calms the acid down."

Ambrose nodded and fled.

Edmund thought the young pilot was probably best left to his own devices. There was time to splash some cool water on his face and slurp down half a cup of tea. He always tried not to drink too much before flying, but the dark, stinging piss that dribbled into the bowl told him he was getting dehydrated. Still, it was hard to get any liquid down. Time for brief comparison of notes with Haddow, who was about to fly, and he was on his own again. They hadn't lost any Hurricanes, and there were claims for half a dozen bombers. The vital thing though, was that they'd turned the attack back before it reached the convoy. In an hour he'd be getting ready to launch again.

With a nod to Ambrose in Red Two, who'd got some colour back in his cheeks, Edmund climbed aboard 6-Z once again. As Charlie helped him with the harness, he tried to calm his breathing, slow his heart. Perhaps that was it. Perhaps the two raids this morning were all the enemy had. Perhaps they'd think better of it.

Bollocks. That was just a taster. The real fight was still coming. The Jerries and Eyeties were testing them, probing the defences.

Alright then. Let's get it done.

Half a dozen fighters were ranged this time. All took off

without incident. Edmund watched the last patrol, Haddow at the head, swinging into the pattern to land. They made the climb quietly, Edmund listening to the sound of his own heart thundering in his ears, feeling each beat pushing against the straps of the Sutton harness. They reached the patrol height, twenty thousand feet, and began to orbit north of the convoy, standing between it and Sardinia.

A rustling sound in his ears was followed by "Attention Red Leader. We have plots all over the board. Reports from half a dozen ships. Large formations coming in from the north, fifty miles out. Angels one-five. Steer three-four-zero. Another flight of six Hurricanes is coming up aft of you."

Edmund acknowledged and slewed his aircraft onto the heading. At this height, the sea below was beginning to fade to grey from its usual blue-black. Easy to spot bombers against. He heard the low-level patrol intercepting a dozen Savoias that seemed to be dropping mines ahead of the convoy. Then another group of torpedo bombers that had cut round to the south. His palms itched with helplessness. Where were their bombers? A couple of minutes had passed, when Ambrose called out "Bandits, eleven o'clock low." He whistled. "Jesus, there must be hundreds of them."

It took Edmund's eyes a couple more seconds to snag the formation, just where the sky faded into the horizon, and then his breath caught. Maybe not hundreds, but seventy or eighty, easily. "This is Red Leader. Large formation of high-level bombers, estimate seventy. Approaching from north. Attacking now. Tally Ho!"

The Hurricanes nosed into a shallow dive and curved round to meet the bombers, face to face. Layers and layers of them, rows and rows. When the formation seemed to crowd the whole sky, Edmund picked a machine right in the middle and gave it a long burst of gunfire, then a shorter one, then pulled up just enough to skim overhead and they were through the first row of bombers and lining up on the second. There was only time for a quick burst and the Hurricanes had broken out of the bottom of the formation. Edmund felt pressure in his chest, realised he'd been holding his breath, released it.

"Red Leader, everyone OK?" Edmund wheezed as he pulled the fighter into a climb. The pilots told off one by one, a couple sounding distant, shaken. "Alright, back in and at 'em."

The Hurricanes sheered to port, holding formation, and rushed down towards the bombers' flank.

There was a sudden clatter, a cacophony of shouts, and "Clyde, behind you!"

Instinctively Edmund shoved the rudder, breaking off the attack and saw a shoal of orange tracers shoot like sparks by the cockpit. A second after that, a plunging shark-form howling by as he hauled back on the spade grip. Jesus, a 110! He kept the Hurricane hard into the turn, glancing in the rear-view mirror every few seconds, each side for beam attacks. When he was satisfied he was clear, he rolled level and surveyed the scene. The huge box formation was behind him, largely intact. His Hurricanes were scattered. Holy Christ, there shouldn't be fighters yet! As long as it was just a few 110s though, that wouldn't be so bad, they just had to watch out. He pulled the Hurricane into a climbing turn, getting himself above the bomber formation.

"Where are you Ambrose," Edmund called. "I'm climbing above the formation, aft of it."

"I see you," his wingman replied, "I'm on your three o'clock."

"Good man, form up, and we'll go again."

"Alright."

The other Hurricane swum up beside him, and took its place on his quarter. Edmund was just about to nose over into a dive when something caught at the edges of his attention. He looked up, where the glare of the sun was just fading, and-

"Jesus! Break, break!" Edmund yelled. "Messerschmitts, loads of the bastards!"

He just had time to turn into the attack, loose off a few rounds, and was swamped in vicious single-seat fighters slicing past him above and below, to either side. There was no time to think, no time to fear, no time to hope. He flipped the Hurricane over onto its back and hauled on the stick, curving through the vertical and levelling out five hundred feet lower. A couple of seconds to drag some air back into his lungs and a decision was made.

He flicked the radio on. "Go for the bombers. Watch out for the fighters, but keep going for the bombers."

There were a smattering of responses, most unintelligible. Edmund checked his mirror, and pushed the throttle through the gate. He was below the bombers now, and swimming up towards them like a shark at a pod of whales. He kept his bursts short, not sure how much ammo he had left, and sprayed two Junkers as he broke through the edge of the formation. The Hurricanes were worrying at the edges, and the huge box had begun to shed little knots of aircraft as the fighters got among them. Then, with a whoop, Haddow was there with the standby flight, pummelling into the bombers from the front and driving right through the middle.

A Messerschmitt 109 slashed past in front of Edmund, and was gone so quickly his thumb hadn't had time to depress the gun button. Where the bloody hell had they come from? Never mind that now.

"Someone get this bastard off me!"

Edmund looked around. That sounded like Ambrose. "Where are you Red Two?"

"Ah... the bombers are above, I'm..." For a second, all Edmund could hear was Ambrose panting. "Towards the convoy. I can't shake him."

Edmund dived, overtaking the bombers, scanning the sky below. There! A Hurricane twisting and jinking, a 109 fixed to its tail, a thread of smoke streaming out somewhere.

"Put her into a tight turn, Ambrose," Edmund shouted. "Break left, now!"

The Hurricane snapped into a bank and arced left, vapour streamers pouring off its wingtips. Edmund reacted just as he did so, getting the nose of his own Hurricane just inside that of the 109. The Messerschmitt's turn began to wash outside, and his tracers went wide. For a moment, the pilot managed to hang with the turn, but Edmund could see it trembling, just the right side of a stall. He was a little too far away still, and his tracers went awry, curving away behind the Messerschmitt's tail. The next burst spattered around the tail, and that was the last of Edmund's ammunition. It was just enough, and the Messerschmitt broke away, diving for the sea.

"He's off you, he's off you," Edmund cried. Ambrose' Hurricane rolled level, and Edmund started looking for the convoy, the carriers.

"Oh, Jesus!"

Edmund's gaze snapped back to the other Hurricane. Smoke was pouring from the cockpit. He saw Ambrose haul the canopy open, and a jet of flame shooting up from below. "Get out! Bail out!" he yelled, but Ambrose was already standing on his seat, the flames blasting around his legs, then he must have pushed the stick forward, as the Hurricane was diving for the sea and a gyrating shape had detached from it, then a white flash and a parachute was opening.

Voice trembling, Edmund called the ADO to send a destroyer, and kept repeating it until someone told him to shut up.

12 August 1942, afternoon

The bombers kept on coming. Edmund and the rest of his section landed, refuelled, rearmed, and launched again straight away. The bombers kept coming. Every time one formation was defeated, another one appeared. The Hurricanes, Martlets and Fulmars kept at them. The merchantman *Deucalion* was hit by a 250kg bomb and began to fall behind the convoy, limping on at a few knots.

Edmund blasted at bombers, dodged fighters, leading a cobbled-together flight. Aircraft were returning riddled with holes. Some weren't returning at all.

And then, just when it seemed the massed waves of bombers would completely overwhelm them, the raids began to ease. By 1500, there were no more large formations of two or three-engined bombers. A gaggle of Heinkels lugging torpedoes tried to break through from astern, and were chased off. A pack of Fiat biplane fighters slashed through at low level and attempted to dive-bomb a merchantman, but missed.

And then, quiet.

The last engine shut off. Edmund closed his eyes. There was nothing but the sound of the sea, the wind, the faint shouts of the maintainers as they marshalled the fighters down below for repairs and replenishment.

"Well Clyde. How was it?" Edmund turned to see Haddow approaching from the island.

"Bloody tiring. Simner's missing. And Ambrose bailed out, I don't know-"

"They picked him up. He's on a destroyer."

Edmund let out an exclamation of sheer relief, almost a bark. "Thank Christ. But he was...there was fire. Is he...?"

"He has burns, yes. But they say he's going to be alright."

"Thank goodness." Edmund took a breath and let it out slowly. "Anyone else still to come in?"

"One or two stragglers I think. Oh, there's a couple now." Haddow pointed to starboard, where a pair of

Hurricanes were treating the carrier to fast pass, showing their topsides to the flight deck, heading aft and carving onto the approach. "How they love to play!"

Edmund shook his head. There was a time and a place for everything! Still, with the relief of the raids ending, he could forgive a 'beat up', just this once.

The Hurricanes were coming in rather oddly though. They had their undercarriage down, but were coming straight in. He'd have to have a word with the pilots if they were from 800. It should have been drummed into any of them that you made a curving approach to keep the batsman in view.

"What on Earth..?" Edmund saw the undercarriage begin to fold up on the fighters, but they were still heading for the deck, picking up speed. "Oh Christ, they're Reggianes! Get down! Everybody get DOWN!"

He flung himself on the deck, hands over his head, and sensed Haddow thumping down beside him. He peered from under his hands just in time to see something detach from each of the fighters and skip on the deck, and pressed his arms over his face again. There was a single thump, a blast of concussion, a tinkle of fragments skittering over the steel flight deck, and the roar of the fighters turning away, belatedly harried by AA fire.

They stood, brushing themselves down. Edmund watched the Reggianes go.

Haddow was panting hard. "Bloody hell, that was-"

There was a wild joy in the CO's eyes which faded, something like puzzlement creeping into its place. Edmund watched as he wobbled, teetered down onto his knees and then onto his back. The entirety of his left side was glossy black. Edmund was on his knees. He put his hand to the darkness. Red, sticky. A stub of torn steel protruded from the wound, incongruous, still warm.

"I-I'll get the MO," Edmund said. "Wait here. I mean. Don't move. It-it'll be OK."

Haddow's hands fluttered at Edmund's chest. "Clyde. Don't go. Don't. Don't go. Don't go."

"All right." He turned his head, feeling even that was a betrayal. "Can somebody get a medic! Quick!" he yelled. The ship was roaring, thundering. Nobody answered.

The surprise in Haddow's face softened, becoming thoughtful. For a moment, two, he was so still that Edmund thought he had already gone, but then his eyes widened a touch again, he looked at Edmund seriously and said "I can't remember what Susan looks like." The thought seemed to distress him more than the shrapnel. "I can't-"

Edmund stared. Haddow would be gone in a moment, he could tell. A few seconds left. "A photo!" he spluttered. "You must have a photo! Let me." The CO's hand flapped weakly at his breast pocket. "I'll get it, Roger. Don't you worry. You know what she looks like. Blonde, and very pretty. Freckles. Green eyes, that...that..." Edmund reached for the pocket, and Haddow's features briefly calmed but before Edmund had undone the button, whatever remained of Haddow at that moment, left.

Men came to take Haddow away. Dimly, in the black depths within him, Edmund knew there were jobs to be done. He would have to report that Haddow had been killed. Killed? He was gone? Impossible. That he, Edmund, was taking command of 800 Squadron. To Wings? Or to the Captain? One or other. Both. As if everything around him were a dream, Edmund began drifting to the island, made his way to the bridge, made his report. Captain Troubridge gazed at him with quiet horror. He looked at his hands, his shirt. He still had Haddow's blood on him.

Edmund left the bridge, still dazed, and wandered. He did not know what to do. What would a CO do in these circumstances? What would Haddow do? Nothing. Haddow was dead. Christ.

"Edmund! There you are. Oh my boy, I'm so sorry."

He looked up. It was Vickery. Vickery. Was he real? The journalist put his arm around his shoulder and started shepherding him, where, he was not sure. After a while Edmund realised they were in the NAAFI. The benches were filled with special dutymen, and stewards were bringing tin mugs around. Vickery took one and passed it to Edmund. He cradled the mug.

"A terrible shame." Vickery shook his head. "It's one thing to be killed in the air, but that... sneak attack."

He raised his eyes slowly. "You saw it?"

"Yes. It had everybody fooled until the last moment."

"I should have seen them sooner."

Vickery shrugged. "If you should, so should everyone."

"We lost people in the air too, you know." Edmund rubbed his face. "Fighters. Up there too. I wasn't expecting them. I should... I should..." He wanted nothing more than to let his head fall forward until it rested on the table. Or to get up, walk to the quarterdeck and jump quietly off the stern.

"Hmm." The journalist nodded slowly. "To tell you the truth, Clyde, it saddens me to see you this way. Holding yourself to impossible standards. You've been through a lot, I know. But when you left Malta you seemed to be surer of yourself."

Edmund dragged his hands through his hair. "On Malta, everything was so simple. Even with...the, uh, characters. Whatever the job happened to be, it was simple."

"And now?"

Edmund shook his head. "I'm responsible. It was my plan. Poor Ambrose..."

"It's just as simple," Vickery said. "Even with men under your command, it's simple. Go up. Fight. You can't protect them all. You can do your level best to protect Malta. For the rest of the day, put everything else out of your mind."

Edmund stared at Vickery. Malta. And Liena. The merchantmen had to get through. Even if all the pilots died, they had to get through. Even if he didn't live to see it.

He felt his blood quicken. "Yes. OK. Right." There were things to do, things to check. A mist seemed to be clearing from his brain. Had to make sure all the possible Hurricanes were available. Re-organise the flights around the remaining pilots. He stood, realised he was holding a mug of tea and gulped it down. It was sugary and strong. The mist had all but gone. "Thanks Vickery."

"My pleasure. I'll see you back here later."

Edmund forced a smile and a nod. He probably wasn't coming back. That was clear now. "Well. We're out of range of Sardinia. But in a couple of hours we'll be in range of Sicily. Don't stick your neck out too much, things might get hairy."

An hour later, with Haddow's writer's help, Edmund had sorted out the squadron. They were four pilots down. Ambrose injured on a destroyer, Simner still missing. Barnes had got hit and crash-landed on *Victorious*. And Haddow. They were also short of aircraft, but the maintainers were doing their best to patch up machines and sling another together from spares.

By 1900 hours, 800 Squadron was able to put eight Sea Hurricanes in the air. It would have to be enough. There was no need for another briefing. Everyone knew what they had to do.

At 1930, the tannoy shrieked. *"Several groups of aircraft approaching from the west. Fighters, stand-to!"*

And then, 6-Z went unserviceable. The engine would not start. Edmund cursed, apologised to Charlie for his harsh words. "How long will it take, do you think?"

"Not long," the rigger replied. "Jamie's changing the plugs. That should sort it."

Brierly, going to his aircraft, stopped. "Everything alright Clyde?"

Edmund growled. Of all the things to happen! "My kite won't start. I'd better take one of the others."

"Don't worry," Brierly said, grinning grimly. "If I'm your senior pilot now, I'd better lead eh? Get your kite fixed. I'll take the standing patrol."

Edmund pressed his hands into his temples. Did it matter? He ought to trust Brierly. He didn't want his first act as CO to be to dismiss a subordinate showing a bit of initiative. "Alright. I'll take the stand-by flight, and I'll be right behind you. Now get going,"

The four Sea Hurricanes roared along the deck and climbed away, their wheels folding sluggishly into their bellies. The next four were ranged. Mechanics crawled over 6-Z, which still had its cowlings off. Edmund looked at his watch. They'd be here any minute.

A ripple of concussion drifted over the water. The destroyers in the outer screen had started to put up a barrage. An engine coughed and roared behind him. He whipped round – 6-Z was running! In the cockpit, Charlie gave him the thumbs up. Edmumd grabbed his Mae West and dashed for the cockpit, shouting to the other three pilots to get off the deck as soon as possible. The first Hurricane ran up its engine, stood on its brakes and roared away. Then the second. The AA barrage was closer, now. The merchantmen had started up, and the cruisers. The third Hurri roared and took off.

He jumped into the cockpit and Charlie helped him with the straps. "Get under cover as soon as you're done here," Edmund yelled over the roar of the engine. "Stay under the armoured deck, alright?"

Charlie nodded and stepped down. The trolley-acc was being disconnected, and in another moment, he had the thumbs up. All set. The barrage was creeping closer. The guns of HMS *Phoebe*, abeam the carrier, bellowed into life. He could actually see the aircraft now, single-engined jobs at about five thousand feet. Just starting to tip over into a dive. Oh, Jesus. Stukas. No time to lose. Edmund set the prop to fine pitch, opened the throttle, let the revs climb and released the brake.

The whole ship seemed to be roaring around him. The AA guns were firing even before he'd left the deck! A scream came from somewhere outside, its intensity rising. As the Hurricane cleared the bow, a vast thunder sounded behind him, and a second later, a tempest bucked the aircraft, whipping it lengthwise as he fought the controls to stay airborne.

The turbulence subsided. Hands shaking, clumsy with urgency, Edmund pulled the undercarriage lever, set the guns, hauled the canopy closed, and banked into a port turn, climbing hard. Looking over his shoulder as the Hurricane swung round, he gasped – *Indomitable* was mantled in smoke, white water billowed off the flight deck. Above him a Stuka, plummeted into view, and with a push on the rudder Edmund lined up the sights and gave it a spray with all twelve guns as it passed across his nose. Then, he kicked the rudder and hauled on the stick, flicking the fighter into a sudden turn, following the dive bomber round. For a second he thought he'd overcooked it and would plummet into the sea, but the wings held their grip on the air, just, and he guided the Hurricane down after the Stuka. Bastard! Bastard! Hot fury vibrated through him, surging through his arms and pouring out and condensing onto the red spot of the gunsight

His tracers flickered all around the aircraft's tail and surely it had wrecked something vital – *burn, you bastard, burn!* – but the bomb detached and with nauseating impotence, Edmund saw it spear towards the carrier. It struck forward of the lift, and plunged through the steel deck as if it were paper. The moments after that were disconnected. An incandescent flash, an instantaneous tornado that seemed to shove the Hurricane fifty feet higher, a ringing in his ears. Out of the fuzz swam the Stuka, recovering from its dive, and skimming across the wavetops. Edmund let out a bellow and grasped the spade grip harder, following the dive bomber, overhauling it inch by inch.

Where seconds before, burning rage dominated, now, Edmund was cold. Icy. Still. The Stuka grew to fill the reflector sight, and though it was still two hundred, a hundred and fifty, a hundred yards away, it felt as though he could reach out and touch the dive bomber's tail, claw through metal with his hands, drag out the pilot who'd done that to his ship and tear him to bloody pieces.

Gradually, he saw the gunner recover from the G of the pull-out, stare in disbelief at the British fighter sitting right on his tail. And then Edmund pushed the gun button. A rain of bullets scythed into the Stuka, chewing patches of the wing into twisted shrapnel, shattering the cockpit hood and riddling the fuselage. The nose dipped, and the Stuka crumpled into the sea at full speed, bursting like a wet paper bag.

He pulled into a tight turn, heading back towards *Indomitable*. His mouth fell open. She seemed to be burning from half a dozen fires, an immense column of black smoke flooding from the hull. At the bow, a chunk of outer plating the size of a hangar door had torn aside and was sticking out like an elephant's ear.

"Where was the blasted low cover?" he snarled at the ADO.

"Out of position, Red Leader," the officer retorted. "Too many plots to cover."

"Can you give me a bearing?"

"Take your pick, Red Leader, the bastards are everywhere."

"Where's my flight, damn you?" Edmund shook his head, checked his six for fighters, and began gaining height. ADO didn't answer. He had to cover the merchant ships. They were the important ones. He turned the Hurricane in their direction, jinking left and right to avoid the AA fire pouring from ships no longer distinguishing between friend and enemy.

He could see knots of aircraft heading for the merchant ships, fighters darting at them. Even then, the defence was starting to break down. He saw a Stuka fleeing at low level pursued by two Martlets. "Let him go, his bomb's already gone," he shouted, but no-one answered him. Had to gain height.

Below, the merchant ships struggled on, bluff bows bulling at the waves. The attacks seemed uncoordinated now – it was already harder to see – but there was a cluster of spots at about angels five, and they were swinging towards the convoy. Edmund looked around. All the other fighters were engaged. He shoved the throttle, snapping the wire, and urged the Hurricane to meet them. Ahead, the low-slung form of the tanker, *Ohio*. The enemy squadron was lining up on it. "Come on, come on!" he shouted at his recalcitrant Hurricane. "Just a bit more speed."

The Stukas were climbing now, having identified their prey, and moving into line-astern. Had they seen him? Didn't matter either way. The lead aircraft was almost at the point of the dive. As Edmund hurtled towards it, he saw the air-brakes open. He pressed the gun button and held it. Incendiaries splashed all around the nose of the Stuka, bursting like firecrackers.

And then a bright flare, a bigger, orange burst and there was nothing left of the aircraft but flaming debris drifting down on the breeze. The following Stukas scattered as if a bomb had gone off among them. A bomb... The gunfire must've set the bomb off. Edmund shrieked with bitter joy.

He saw the dive bombers jettison their bombs on empty sea, and turn tail. The Hurricanes fell on them. Soon there were a dozen columns of smoke issuing from burning wrecks on the water. A few had escaped though. He saw them wave-hopping away, back to their island, the cowards.

Bastards! He set off after them, opening fire at extreme range, desperate to claim one more for the murder of his shipmates.

And then, he remembered Vickery. That calm voice. It seemed to cut through the blood thundering in his ears. Malta. That was all that mattered. Vickery, who might have been blown to smithereens a moment ago. He'd still say that.

"Anyone need any help?" he called, wading back into

the fight over the convoy. Some of the Hurricanes and Fulmars were tangling with fighters. Others trying to head off the few remaining Stukas that hadn't made an attack yet. Steadily, they drove each one off.

"Got a sticky one on my tail!" someone shouted, "Can't get shot of him."

Edmund recognised Brierly's voice. There he was, caught in a circling duel with a Macchi 202. Edmund hauled his Hurricane in behind it and latched onto the fighter's tail, giving the other Hurricane pilot a chance to make a break for it. It was as though the gunsight had a magnet in it, drawing itself irresistibly onto the Macchi, which flicked, yo-yoed, zigged and zagged. A harsh joy built in Edmund's chest, bursting out into a savage cry. Heightening desperation seemed to radiate from the Macchi. It was at his mercy. And then the fighter dived for the sea, levelled off at a few feet above the wavetops and began racing for home.

Edmund followed the fighter for a few miles, making sure it didn't double back and claim one last kill. But he did not open fire. After all, what would the point be? And it might even be the pilot who had declined to kill him off Malta when Edmund was a sitting duck. He sensed it was not – a rookie perhaps, experiencing combat for the first time today. It was a gift to his saviour nonetheless. A tiny scrap of mercy in this charnel house.

Sicily appeared as a smudge on the distant horizon, and he finally felt able to draw breath. What to do? For a second, a determination fizzed through him, to carry on, ever forward, back to that Luftwaffe base he'd shot up a few weeks ago. Blaze through the last of the ammo and then dive the Hurricane onto a hangar. The thought passed in an instant, leaving no more than a residue of nausea.

Well. That was that. It was over. Edmund shivered, a spasm of it rippling from his feet to his head. Jesus, it was cold. What the hell was the time, anyway? It must be after 2000. The sky above was a peaceful, royal blue, turning greyish towards the horizon, where to the west it faded into tobacco-stain yellow and to the east, the almost-black of wine. Edmund exhaled, jetting steam into the cockpit, coating the gunsight with fog. He'd done all he could. All anyone could. It was up to others now.

Time to go home. He reversed course, banking to port, and his chest caught. The sea below was an inky nothingness. In complete shadow already. He couldn't make out a thing down there. He scanned up to the horizon, then banked to starboard and did the same. Nothing. No ships. No sign of the distant coastlines. Just a sheet of black that the sky sank into on all sides.

It was alright though. He could call the controller. They'd direct him to a deck.

He toggled the radio. "Red Leader requesting a bearing."

Nothing but a faint hiss.

"Red Leader, requesting a bearing. Pedestal, can you hear me? Acknowledge please."

For some reason at that moment Godden leapt back into his head. Godden, last seen flying out into the Mediterranean, duped by a false radio signal from Sicily. At that moment, Edmund would have given anything just for that fake controller's voice telling comforting lies. The comfort of contact with another human, even one who was trying to kill him. But even Sicily remained silent.

It was an odd thought. He couldn't think of Godden as dead. Couldn't imagine the moment when his fuel must have run low, and, seeing nothing but dark waters all around, he had put his Hurricane down on the surface, whooshing into the sea with a gut-tearing lurch and a struggle out onto the wing... Or bailed out, splashing down beneath his parachute. No, to Edmund it was as though Godden were still out there. Still up here, flying on into nothingness. Engine a constant drone, blue above, blue below. Maybe that was what it was like. Maybe you didn't know you were dead, you just kept on going.

No, idiot. There would be a smashing, a rending of metal and bone, a tearing of fabric and flesh, a boiling of solid water and the last moments would be violent and short.

And just for a second, that was alright too. It would be an end to it. A rest, of thoughts.

No! It was as if another voice had shouted in his head, and he started, jolting against the harness. No. This need not be the end. Should not. He had more fight left in him, damn it, and once that was done, if he was still around, he would get to find peace.

And somehow, he would get back to Malta. Find Liena. Even if it was just for one more walk around Valetta. And then, after the war, if there was an after, he would tell of all this in poetry. Sing those lives, even if no-one was listening. Haddow, Charlie, Geoff, the boys on Malta, Cocke and Godden. Barbara, of course, Vickery. And Liena, always Liena.

"Le vent se lève. Il faut tenter de vivre."
The wind rises. We must try to live.

His favourite poem. It had been with him all along.

He let out a long sigh, and a little of the stress of the last few days seemed to ebb away with it.

To live, then. To live, whatever happened.

Easier said than done. With the decision, the first twang of panic. With an effort of will, Edmund pushed it aside.

He was still flying the reciprocal of the track he'd flown out on. How many gallons left? Damn, but it was hard to see the instruments. He stretched forward against the harness. Fifteen or so. Quarter of an hour's flying. He needed to let down, whether or not he knew where he was going. Good God, he wouldn't even know when he was about to hit the water. The altimeter wasn't as precise as all that.

It was the confounded dusk, this neither one thing nor the other light. If it would just get fully dark then he could at least see the instruments properly. But then he'd never have a hope of finding the carrier again. Not even the whole convoy. He closed his eyes for a second, fixing his position against that where the convoy had last been on an imaginary map, heading in that direction.

Come on, think! Think! He needed to lose height at any rate, at point he estimated he was roughly over the convoy – assuming it had not changed speed or course in the last ten minutes, or he'd misremembered or miscalculated – he throttled back and eased into a standard rate turn, gradually dropping towards the gaping maw of the sea. For the moment it was all he could do, and the thought gave him a second or two's calm before the terror rushed back into him, choking his chest, buzzing in his arms, turning his guts to water.

Edmund glanced at the horizon, and for a second could make no sense of its indistinctness. And then realised, *blast*, the canopy was fogging up. He changed hands on the spade grip and dug into his pocket for a handkerchief. It just smeared the condensation around. Come on Edmund, this was basic. He pulled the canopy back an inch and locked it. Even opened just a crack, the slipstream burst into the cockpit, a jet catching his eyes and making them water half a second before he remembered to put his goggles on. He could have laughed. Get a bloody grip, he told himself, you're acting like a tyro.

As the Hurricane dropped inexorably downwards, it was falling deeper into shadow. The glimmer of radium dials and needles swum out of the shade. Well that was something. Now lights. He reached for the switch, barked his knuckles on something unexpected, and walked his fingers across the panel until they found the right toggle. One red star and one green winked into being at the wingtips.

Perhaps he'd be able to see smoke against the paler sky to westward when he got low enough.

Just as he had solved one problem, another leapt out. A lazy stream of green tracer arced up towards the Hurricane and bowled past. Another joined it. Jesus! They were shooting at him! Somewhere among the tumble of confusion and anger came a dart of joy. He was above the convoy! But they were shooting at him!

Well they did that even when they could see what they were supposed to be shooting at. Couldn't they tell from his IFF? Well, only the ships with radar, which wasn't most of them. What about his navigation lights then? No enemy would be flying around lit up like Christmas! He fumbled with the R/T switch again, "Hello this is Red Two, for Christ's sake can you tell them to stop shooting at me!" But again there was only the shush of static. Either his radio was faulty or theirs was. Or, he considered with a prickling that darted across his skin, the fighter direction ships had all been sunk.

Then how...?

Ah, recognition. Flares.

The lever was aft of the trim control. He fumbled for it, knocking his fingers on half a dozen projections until he found it. Select a colour. What were the colours of the day? Green, red, green wasn't it? Damn, damn, they were still firing. At least the whole damned fleet hadn't started up yet. He must be silhouetted against the western sky for at least some of the ships. Perhaps if he put his landing gear down they'd see he was trying to land? No, they'd probably just mistake the Hurri for a Stuka. Come on Edmund, colours! He could not see the markings on the slot in the gloom. Why couldn't he remember where the colours were. No good staring right at it. Just look a bit off centre, and...there! He pushed the selector to green and pushed it to fire. Then red, and fire, and green again. Some of the streams of tracer sputtered out. One or two kept going, but they weren't terribly accurate, and soon he passed beyond their range.

It was one thing to find the convoy. Quite another to find a deck to land on. And land on it.

Would they be at night stations yet? A chill ran through him. What if the escort had already detached? What time was it? Damn it, he might only have minutes to get down. And with the AA fire stopping, he was once again no longer entirely sure where the ships were.

What was his altitude? Coming down through two thousand feet. He swallowed, his throat feeling as though it had a rock in it. A big, dry rock. Point blank range for any trigger-happy gunner. He edged the throttle forward and lessened the descent. By now he could hear his heart beating. It thumped against his earphones.

Oddly, it didn't seem so dark now. His eyes must have adjusted a little. There was the silhouette of a merchantman ahead and to port...and another. He was inside the destroyer screen. But which side? The carriers would be in the space in the middle. Carrier, he reminded himself. Just *Victorious* left now. It would be a miracle if *Indom* was still afloat. Even if she was, there would be no landing on her ravaged deck.

God, he hoped everyone had got off her alright.

Fumbling like a blindfolded man, he moved from ship to ship, trying to read the shape of the convoy, edging in what should be the right direction. There was the second column. Good. Edmund felt his shoulders relax slightly. Now he was certain where he was. Less chance that he'd lose sight of the ships and not be able to find them again. Fuel? About eight minutes. Less than ten at any rate. The escort would be astern of the merchantmen. It was enough, just. Just pray there was enough wind over the deck.

Carefully, carefully, he circled to port, keeping the ships in view through the murk, until he was drifting downrange. In a moment or two the escort should be in sight, if they were still attached. What was the time? Surely they were about to depart at any moment? Can't worry about that now. Just find *Victorious* and put her down. If the escort's gone...well, just have to hope they haven't.

A creamy slash of wake bisected the canopy to starboard. He followed it to the head, where a dark mass resolved itself into the form of a cruiser. Looked like a Dido-class... yes, he was sure of it. An AA cruiser meant the carriers must be near. Another line of wake scoring across the sea...another Dido. And astern of her... Yes! Thank the Lord, a carrier! His whole chest was vibrating with stress, his heart beating time. Which carrier? If by some miracle *Indom* was still afloat, he couldn't land on her, not the state her deck would be in. Edmund peered through the gloom, trying to pick out anything that might mark the carriers apart. Something looked not right about this one... Yes, it was listing. And that haze around the after section was smoke. It was *Indom*! Still afloat! Still moving! He rocked the Hurricane's wings as he passed, hoping someone would see. Perhaps Vickery. "Hold on old girl," he muttered, not sure whether he was talking to the carrier or his aircraft. He hoped Vickery had survived. And Charlie, and the others.

Fuel? Less than five minutes. He wouldn't get a second attempt.

And there! *Victorious*, a blocky bulk against the southern

sky. He banked towards her, pulling the undercarriage lever as he did so, guiding the fighter as close as he dared down the carrier's starboard flank. Please someone, for goodness' sake, take note of what he was doing.

Hands shaking. He released his right hand from the spade grip, flexed the fingers, wiped them on his shorts, repeated the process with his left. He'd need to be precise. He banked gently to starboard, counted to ten, pulled the canopy back and lowered the flaps.

The roar of the wind in the cockpit was explosive, freezing. Edmund's eyes were glued to the turn and bank indicator and the altimeter. Mustn't lose it now. Pain started to bloom in his chest. Hard to get enough air into it. He gulped a burning lungful. The gyro drifted on round.

Now. He must be heading for *Victorious,* more or less. Oh, thank the lord, they'd switched the homing light on! The lamp at the masthead gleamed beautifully. The Hurricane crawled closer. There was a floodlight on the after deck too now. But he was drifting off to port. Jesus, they were out of wind. Fifteen degrees or so. He put on a bit of rudder, but the Hurricane didn't crab too well. Christ. Edmund see-sawed the fighter down towards the deck. One hundred and fifty feet. One hundred. Hope the wires are up. Bats had torches in his hands. Oh, good man Bats! Port, port... Starboard. Too high. Too high. Just about right. Just about... The acres of steel plate rushed upwards... The wires like dark stripes across it, and he chopped the throttle, and he was going to make it, but he wasn't straight.

Thu-thuk hammered through the airframe and Edmund's

head drove forward. The Hurricane lurched, and seemed to be stopping, but in a moment something under the seat gave, and the fighter lunged to the right. A fusillade rattled out ahead, the prop striking the deck, and in a spray of sparks the Hurricane with Edmund in it, skittered towards the carrier's looming island. He released the spade grip, and an instant later, everything was engulfed in noise and incandescence.

A second later, and the Hurricane was silent, still. Edmund shook his head. Looked at his arms in wonder. One of them felt wet. Was this...? The Hurricane was on its nose, leaning to starboard. Just beyond the cockpit was the wreck of another Hurricane. It was parked abaft the island, and he'd smashed into it. Jesus.

There was a welter of clanking, rattling, odd yells outside, and a figure appeared out of the night, throwing its arms into the cockpit. "Are you hurt? Are you hurt? Can you get out?"

Edmund turned his head towards the noise, the nonsensical figure. It meant him. He nodded, tried to speak, but his lips wouldn't form words. Swollen. Must have hit his face on something.

"Need to get you out sir, fire," the figure said. Out. Yes, of course. He flapped his hands at the harness, managed to get the pin out. The straps fell away and he felt hands on his shoulders. His legs were kicking, and after a moment he persuaded them to push him up, as he scrabbled with his arms to find purchase, but there were more hands, heaving his arms, and he was out of the Hurricane and running, staggering, falling, crawling. Now he could hear the crackling, see the glow of the flames, and he tried to turn to look at his Hurricane, to see if it would be all right, but the hands kept pushing, heaving, until his legs would not keep up and he fell to his knees on the deck. He realised the blood dripping onto the steel was his own, and then the night closed around him, the noise and glare fading mercifully away.

25 August 1944

Valetta. The last time Edmund had been here, he had got himself horribly lost. But also, he reflected, found. This time there was no mistake and he had his bearings. He found Kingsway – *Strada Reale* as Liena called it, and as it was in his mind – and began walking up it. It was much as he remembered. A row of grand buildings stretching away, ruler-straight, punctuated by gaps like mute mouths. Only a couple more gaps since '42. Most of the heaps of rubble had been cleared. The biggest difference was the hundreds of sailors and soldiers milling or striding purposefully around. Valletta did not have the haunted feeling it had before, the air of a city staring destruction in the face. The war raged on, but Malta had already won its battle. As he moved up the street, Edmund wondered what Malta would be like in the years to come. He could feel the determination pulsing in the very stones. Malta would rebuild. And no longer as a fortress. It could begin to live freely again.

As he reached the square, Edmund could not help but take a moment to gaze on the ruined opera house, roofless, shattered, somehow more majestic than a complete building would have been with its pillars now supporting nothing but the sky whence their near-destruction had arrived.

Edmund meandered around it, drifting through the crowds, aware he was early but unwilling to wander too far away. Astonishingly, he felt his heart begin to thump and smiled at the silliness of it. As he continued along his circuit of the opera house, he started to look for a very particular block of stone. Perhaps it had been cleared away as rubble. It surely would be sooner or later, and that would be a pity, but at least let it be here for now.

Ah yes, there it was. With a swell of disappointment that passed almost immediately he realised there were already people sitting on it. Two women, one civilian, the other in a dark uniform, in earnest conversation with each other. He drew closer, not wanting to intrude, unable to pull himself away from the spot. He wanted to meet Liena here. He didn't want it to be anywhere else.

"...Things seem to be winding down here, don't they?" the uniformed woman was saying. "Feels as though the worst will be over soon."

"Hmm," said the other, "perhaps. To me it feels busier than before. More ships coming and going. Many more. Lots to organise. No air raids to worry about these days, but plenty more fighting. Greece. The islands. Yugoslavia."

"Yes, I s'pose. But that's just mopping up. There's a lot less for me to do in the signals biz. No, I think I'm going to move on. Go where I'm most needed."

The civilian woman laughed. "And you can just snap

your fingers and go where you like."

The Wren laughed too. "Well, it's not as easy as all that, but I have a talent for making myself indispensable." She leaned in and lowered her voice. "I'm learning Japanese, you know. First step, get myself out to Ceylon. Then perhaps Australia. Then we'll see. That's where the real work will be."

"I have enough *real* work trying to find accommodation for all these new arrivals," replied the civilian. She swept her arm at the uniformed mass blundering through the square. "It's worse than when King George came. Ah! As if we didn't have enough to worry about."

"Well. I hear rumours of another terribly important person coming here soon," the Wren said, conspiratorially. "Some wretched war hero."

"Oh? We don't know anything about that kind of thing on Malta!"

"He sounds frightfully boring. He's got his own Seafire squadron apparently. I hear he's very nearly an ace."

Edmund chuckled. "Hellcat squadron, actually, appropriately enough. Hello Barbara. How long have you known I was here?"

She turned to him and grinned. "Only a moment. I'd recognise that shadow anywhere. You really should learn to stop slouching. And who else wears their cap straight?"

He nodded to Liena, feeling himself smiling despite his efforts to keep his face still. She rolled her eyes, but smiled too. "Spies get shot around here, you know," she chided.

"Everywhere I go, people want to shoot me," he sighed. "I'm beginning to wonder if it's something I said."

"I'd start to worry if anyone *didn't* want to shoot you." Barbara stood, smoothing the skirts of her uniform. She nodded at Edmund and Liena in turn. "I'll leave you two to it then." They began to protest, but she held her hand up. "No, you don't need me hanging around while you get reacquainted. Besides, I've a date with a book. Japanese doesn't learn itself, you know. Oh," she nodded at Edmund, "Mr Vickery sends his best."

Barbara turned and in a moment she was lost in the crowd. Edmund looked at Liena and she returned his gaze, unreadable for a moment, and then stepped to his side and slipped her arm through his. It felt as though two long-separated pieces of a jigsaw had just slotted back together.

"You and Barbara getting along alright then I see," he said. "How did you meet her?"

"At the Bastion, at first" Liena replied. "She needed someone to help her organise billets, for the Wren radio mechanics. Lots of them coming in now."

It was a small island, after all. For no reason that Edmund could identify, the idea of Barbara and Liena becoming such firm friends was intensely satisfying.

They started walking, in no direction in particular, allowing themselves to be guided by the crowd. After what felt somehow like moments and hours had passed, Edmund realised they were heading in the direction of the Lascaris Bastion and the Barrakka. It took a good long while, weaving between knots of servicemen and civilians. But they had time. Eventually, having exchanged not a single word since leaving the opera house, they found themselves above the battery, looking out over the glittering harbour, the disarmed battleships of the Italian fleet, the rakish British destroyers.

At some unspoken signal, they looked at each other. Liena frowned, reached out and with the tips of her fingers, brushed the scar that slanted across his right cheekbone, down toward his mouth. "It must have been bad," she murmured.

Edmund shrugged. "It's alright now." He turned towards the anchorage again. One of those destroyers was HMS *Hindscarth*, the ship that had brought him here before. He hoped the crew from that day had made it this far.

"How long?" asked Liena, almost too softly to be heard.

"A few days."

"Then what?"

"Then I go where the real work is."

She hugged his arm tighter.

"Long enough for me to talk to a priest," he added.

He felt, rather than saw her smile. It seemed to ripple through her. "Good," she said, "but we can think about that tomorrow." They turned back to the harbour, over which the sun was starting to set, a red ball throwing its rays over the ranks of warships, and her hand twined into his.

Author's note

Operation 'Pedestal' – the 'Santa Maria convoy' – is probably the most famous single convoy of the Second World War, and one of the most significant, so it was important to do it justice in this fictional version.

As in the preceding two novellas, 'Harpoon' and 'Bastion', I have tried to stay close to the historical events, partly out of respect to the people who were there, but mostly because the truth of these events is just as dramatic as fiction. The timetable of the convoy is real, as are incidents such as the French airliner that spotted the convoy but was spared, and the raids on it are as reported in contemporary accounts. In writing the battles and the events that led up to them, I am indebted to the Armoured Carriers website – www.armouredcarriers.com – which compiles a wealth of primary source material about Operation 'Pedestal' and all the activities of the Royal Navy's armoured fleet carriers in WW2. It is highly recommended. Many books have covered 'Pedestal' over the years, and it would be hard to narrow it down to a few recommendations, but Peter C Smith's Pedestal: The Convoy That Saved Malta, and Richard Woodman's Malta Convoys 1940-43 are an excellent place to start.

A few small alterations to the history were made, chiefly to reflect as wide an experience of the convoy as possible in a book with a single point of view. The raid by two Reggiane fighters posing as Hurricanes by entering the landing pattern, then dropping anti-personnel bombs, took place, but the attack was made on HMS *Victorious* rather than *Indomitable*, and no-one was killed (though several later reports indicated otherwise). In reality, the heavy escort turned back on the 12th before darkness fell, but Edmund's last-minute landing on *Victorious* is based on the experience of pilots who were flying late on the 11th, when a late raid left several fighters in the air at nightfall. Most of the characters are fictional, but Dickie Cork, senior pilot of 880 Squadron, is real. Cork was one of the leading Fleet Air Arm fighter pilots of the war, and became an 'ace in a day' during Pedestal, shooting down five enemy aircraft. There really was a converted RAF Hurricane Mk II used during the operation – BD771, '7-Z' was with 880 Squadron.

Heartfelt thanks go to JA Ironside for reading and commenting on a draft, and to Richard and Tara at Sharpe books, and everyone who has worked on this series. It's an honour to see it in print with such beautifully designed covers.

Any interested readers are very welcome to find me on Twitter – look for @navalairhistory – and on my blog Naval Air History at navalairhistory.com

Printed in Great Britain
by Amazon